Alonzo W. Slayback

A Memorial Volume

being selections in poetry and prose

Alonzo W. Slayback

A Memorial Volume
being selections in poetry and prose

ISBN/EAN: 9783337369897

Printed in Europe, USA, Canada, Australia, Japan

Cover: Foto ©Andreas Hilbeck / pixelio.de

More available books at **www.hansebooks.com**

A

MEMORIAL VOLUME:

BEING SELECTIONS

IN POETRY AND PROSE

From the Written Thoughts of

COL. ALONZO W. SLAYBACK,

Including a Brief

BIOGRAPHICAL SKETCH.

ST. LOUIS, MO.:

J. H. CHAMBERS & CO., 405 North Third Street,

1883.

ERRATA.

———

Page 56, 5th line from top..................................· *speeds* not *spreads.*
  "   57, 1st line from top .... *ye* not *we.*
  "   57, 3rd line from top ....*the* not *thy.*
  "   92, after 1st line, insert................*"Brought them back to dawn."*
  "   93, 4th line from bottom...........................*adored* not *deplore.*
  " 100, 5th line from bottom.............................*thine* not *there.*
  " 125, 5th line from top .... *Well!* not *Nell!*
  " 126, 5th line from top........................*my lonely* not *her lovely.*
  " 152, 3rd line from top.........................*Spurned* not *Scorned.*
  " 156, 7th line from top................................. *One* not *The.*
  " 170, 13th line from top ....*Hood* not *Wood.*
  " 193, after 5th verse of poem, insert:

> " But cheers arose, and found his voice,
> The multitude expressed their choice
> In tones so plain, that rake began
> To swear he'd rule all or none."

Page 194, 1st line 2d verse.............................. ....*Like* not *The.*
  " 201, 8th line from top..*Y* not *Z.*
  " 203, 1st line...........................*All mouldy* not *He moulded.*
  " 213, 2nd line from top ....*hues* not *lines.*
  " 216, 7th line from bottom...........................*freemen* not *foemen.*
  " 218, 2nd line from top......................*thirsty bird* not *little bird.*
  " 225, 2nd line from top.............................*summed* not *summon.*
  " 237, 3rd line from top.................................*Four* not *For.*

CONTENTS.

Col. Slayback's widow has here put into permanent form many of the lyrics which he left behind; not only to do honor to her husband's memory, but to give pleasure to his many friends who crave copies.

Some of these poems have been printed before; but only a very few were intended for publication. They are but the sparkles of his life, translated into language—written, because the feeling of the moment moved him to catch the fleeting fancy, and fasten it in his flight.

Simply,

"He sat him down, and seized a pen, and traced
Words"—

which open windows of the soul, through which one may look into a heart that moved from deeper depths than the world supposed.

They date from boyhood, and run along with all the years of his unfinished life. Love and philosophy, faith and whimsy, the grave and the gay, will all be found here: and they help to show the sunlight that shone upon his daily path; or to picture the shadows that drifted by in quicker, or more stately measure, as the clouds that made them, gathered within the sphere of his most sensitive nature, to settle for a time, or to lift away as quickly as they came. To all emotions he was ever ready to respond—and these their voicings are his antiphons.

Many who knew him less intimately than those to whom he opened all his heart, will be surprised to find upon these pages a revelation of great tenderness of spirit; while all will recognize the frankness of the bold and honest heart, which knew no fear. A profound reverence, as well, displays itself for sacred things.

These memorials of the man will be gladly welcomed by his comrades, and his friends, now that he has passed forever

> "Beyond the frost chain, and the fever,
> Beyond the rock waste, and the river,
> Beyond the ever, and the never."

P. G. R.

Biographical Sketch.

The writer responds with all the warmth of friendship to Mrs. Slayback's request to contribute a biographical sketch of her husband, to be published with his poems, and yet it is a duty not easily performed.

To undertake the analysis and portrayal of the character of any man, in a few pages, is a vain attempt—how much more so in the case of one as gifted as Alonzo W. Slayback. Only the salient facts of his life will therefore be presented; assured that the reader will generously appreciate the marked characteristics which made his career brilliant, endeared him to his friends, and commanded the respect of his opponents.

He is pronounced by all who knew him to have

been a noble man, full of generous impulses, brilliant in intellect, brave in danger, courageous under trial, and tender as a woman in his sympathies; abounding in charity, munificent in gifts; a true and steadfast friend.

Alonzo William Slayback was born July 4, 1838, at Plum Grove, Marion County, Mo., the homestead of his maternal grandfather. He was a direct descendant, on his mother's side, of the Countess Susanna Lavillon and Bartholemi Dupuy, Royal Guardsman to Louis XIV., whose tragic persecution, marvelous escape from France and safe arrival on the shores of Virginia, are familiar to the lover of history. The revocation of the Edict of Nantes gave birth to the romantic career of those two renowned Huguenots, Bartholemi Dupuy and Jacques de la Fontaine.

On reaching Virginia, in 1700, Bartholemi Dupuy joined the Fontaines and Trabues, friends who had preceded him, settling in Manakin Town, on the banks of the James river, where he resided until his death. When dying, he bequeathed to his eldest son Jacques the triangular sword which had served him in fourteen battles in Flanders, and his son at Guilford Court-House, and it still remains a legacy in his family in Virginia.

The maternal grandparents of Alonzo W. Slayback were Jeremiah A. Minter (who still lives, at the age of 86) and Sallie Minter (nee McDowell), both of Kentucky. Sallie McDowell's father was a son of Colonel Samuel McDowell, an officer of the American army in the war of the Revolution. The McDowells were of Scotch descent. His paternal great-grandfather, Solomon Slayback, was a soldier under Washington— one of the Jersey recruits from near Princeton, N. J. Originally the Slaybacks were from Amsterdam, Holland. Dr. Abel Slayback, of Cincinnati, Ohio, was the son of Solomon Slayback and father of Alexander Lambdin Slayback, of whom the subject of this sketch was the eldest child. Thus it is seen he was descended from patriots on both sides, and the noble characteristics of his ancestors shone out grandly in him.

The father of A. W. Slayback was a lawyer. He removed to Lexington, Mo., and died at the early age of thirty years, leaving a widow and four children, three sons and one daughter.

The early education of the children was conducted by the mother. To her judicious training Alonzo was greatly indebted for the true development of the native elements of character that made him a peer among men.

Having completed his preparatory studies, he was placed at the age of ten in the Masonic College, then presided over by that distinguished divine, Rev. Adiel Sherwood, D. D., where he pursued a full collegiate course, graduating June, 1856, at eighteen, with the first honors in a class of seven. His earliest ambition was to become a lawyer, and during the last four years of his college course his studies were directed to this end. After leaving college, he went to St. Joseph, Mo., where he alternately taught school and studied law. This early struggle, with its wholesome experiences, served to bring out his native energy, quicken his assiduity, and develop that self-reliance which was a material factor in lifting him to the fame and position he so justly won. In September, 1857, he was admitted to practice by Judge Norton at St. Joseph. Here he enjoyed the friendship of two very estimable men, Bela M. Hughes (with whom he studied law) and the Rev. A. V. C. Schenck — diverse in their character, yet both noble and worthy men. Their influence had much to do in shaping the young lawyer's mental and moral nature. His first law partner was Joseph P. Grubb, now judge of the Circuit Court, Buchanan County Circuit. He was married April 14, 1859, to Miss Alice A. Waddell, daughter of Wm. B. Waddell, of Lexington.

In the war between the States he enlisted in the Confederate service. Born on Southern soil, surrounded from childhood with Southern influences and habits, loving his native section with an ardor that outstripped his love of life, he did not hesitate for a moment, but promptly took the side that to him was right. In June, 1861, he joined the command of Gen. Sterling Price. In July, venturing in from the camp to see his wife, the house was surrounded and he was taken prisoner, and put on a boat at the river until the fort at Masonic College was finished, to which the prisoners were afterwards removed. After he had been in prison three weeks,

he asked the guard to accompany him to the
spring near the fort. The prisoner carried a
bucket, and the guard his gun. At the spring
the guard, thinking his prisoner was stooping to
get water, was unprepared for the blow the young
man gave him with the bucket. Mr. Slayback,
knowing every inch of the ground from childhood,
ran quickly down the hill, and escaped the bullets
that were sent after him by the astonished guards.
Wandering through the woods during the night,
he reached the house of Mrs. Young the next
morning, who gave him shoes and socks, and a
horse for his journey. After the battle at Lexington in September, 1861, he was elected Colonel
of the Missouri Volunteers, and commissioned by
Gov. Caleb Jackson. When General Price was
ordered into the regular service of the Confederacy east of the Mississippi river, Col. Slayback
enlisted for " three years or during the war."

Soon after he was appointed Capt. of Ordnance
under Gen. Martin E. Green.

At the battle of Elkhorn he was assigned the
command of a regiment hastily called together,
made up partly of State volunteers and of Con-

federate troops. In this engagement Col. Slayback and his men did good service. They were then tranferred east of the Mississippi line, and he was promoted for meritorious conduct at Corinth and Farmington. He was ordered west of the Mississippi again, to recruit with Col. Waldo P. Johnson and other officers, and to report to Gen. Hindman, who assigned him to duty with the calvary at the front. When starting on Shelby's raid into Missouri, he was taken sick and left behind. During the month of November, 1863, Mrs. Slayback, who was with her father at Lexington, heard from some of the returned soldiers that her husband had been left by Shelby's command in Boston Mountains, dying with typhoid fever.

She decided to leave home, friends and her young child, to go to him. Federal bayonets, untried dangers, grave difficulties, all were powerless to alter the determination of the wife to reach her husband. Refused a permit to pass the Federal lines, she was compelled to accept "banishment papers," which she did without hesitation. Death only could keep her from ministering to her husband's comfort in his sickness. In company with Mrs. Isaac Ruffner, she landed at Napoleon, Arkansas, and by the kind assistance of a gentleman travelling the same way, after many hardships, reached Washington, Ark., only to find that Col. Slayback had been removed to Shreveport, La. Following on as quickly as possible, Col. Cundiff conducted Mrs. Slayback to the hospital, where she found her husband, unable to lift his head from the pillow. The soldier rallied under the inspiration of his wife's presence. He was soon removed to Dr. Newman's, in Caddo parish, and in three months was nursed back to life and hope.

In March, 1864, Gen. E. Kirby Smith, Commander of the Trans-Mississippi Department, made Col. Slayback bearer of special dispatches to Richmond, to the Secretary of War, Gen. Seddon, who commanded Gen. Smith to assign Capt. Slayback to duty in the line. By order of Gen. Smith he recruited a regiment of cavalry in Southeast Missouri, of which he was elected Colonel. This regiment, "The Slayback Lancers," was attached to Shelby's old brigade, and so remained until the close of the war.

When it was known that Gen. Robt. E. Lee had surrendered at Appomattox, Gens. Price and Shelby decided to go into Mexico. Col. Slayback joined them. The cause for which he had fought and which he believed to be just, the cause he had loved and so nobly defended, was lost. He felt he had no country, no home, and he determined to seek one in a foreign land. Forty-eight of his old command chose to share his fortunes. They formed themselves into a company, electing him Captain, and joined Gen. Shelby's expedition into Mexico.

The expedition crossed the Rio Grande at Piedras Negras, in Mexico, where, on the 4th of July, 1865, they buried, in the waters of the swift rolling river, the last Confederate flag that floated to the breeze.

Col. Slayback, on reaching Lampasas, Mexico, was again overtaken by a violent sickness. Recovering after an illness of several days, he pursued his way to Monterey, which he reached July 11th, where he remained until Sept. 16th, when he set out for the city of Mexico per diligence, stopping on his way at San Luis Potosi and several other minor towns.

He reached the city Oct. 8th. Here he was
again taken sick, and lay for some days at the
San Carlos Hotel. Gen. Thomas O'Horan, Pre-
fect of the city of Mexico under Maximilian,
hearing of the Colonel's condition, kindly sent
his carriage and removed him to his residence,
thirteen miles from the city, where every attention possible was bestowed on the distinguished
American. Here Col. Slayback remained until
January 23rd, 1866, enjoying the hospitality of
this noble gentleman, and perfecting himself in
Spanish.

Throughout his stay in Mexico, the Colonel
kept a regular journal of his life, in the shape
of letters to his absent wife—letters replete with
love and devotion, interspersed with vivid de-
scriptions of scenes and scenery through which
he had passed; and of facts and records of
the war, comments on men he had met, friends
he had made and from whom in sadness he had
parted. Colonel Slayback was one of the few
busy men who found time to keep a full diary of
his life.

Just here we make a few extracts from his

journal: "Now in the meantime I am uneasy about Ma. In a New Orleans *Picayune* of Jan. 14th I find, among the names of passengers who sailed the day before, 'Mrs. A. L. Slayback,' on board the British steamer Caroline, Capt. Hainby, Also Capt. Heber Price, who is at Carlotta, the colonial village, has received a letter from Misouri for his father the General, which is marked 'favor of Mrs. Slayback,' and mailed at Havana. I am puzzled over all this, but cannot doubt that Ma is on her way in quest of me, and has probably stopped at Havana, hearing of my improved health."

Leaving the city of Mexico Jan. 26th, he visited the Confederate colony at Cordova under Gens. Price and Shelby. Under date Feb. 9th he says: "I stopped to see how my American friends were prospering, and remained at the house of Gen. Shelby, where I feel very much at home. Mrs. S. and the children are here, and the General seems contented : is opening a farm, preparing to plant coffee and sugar, cotton and rice. The plantain and banana, with their broad tropical leaves and delicious clusters of fruit—the oranges and lemons, the mango and lime, pine-apple and palm—fill the air with delicious odors, and offer to the sight a constant variety of romantic and interesting scenery. As I came along the road the last morning I noticed the laborers gathering a red berry that looked like cranberries, and saw them drying them in the sun on mats—afterwards collected in dark, withered heaps in their huts. I did not find out until I got here that this berry is the savory coffee, the beverage of the world. I shall go down to Vera Cruz to-morrow, and hasten to Havana as soon as possible."

"Vera Cruz, Feb. 3. The America packet came in sight within an hour after we arrived, but will not sail on the 5th, its regular day, and shall have to *wait* again for the Spanish steamer, which sails on the 6th, and then takes six days to go through to Havana. This delay I submit to with a poor grace, for I have received positive news that Ma is at Havana awaiting me; and my impatience, in the first place, to relieve her anxieties, and, secondly, to *see* her, knows no bounds. She has sent me a certificate of deposit for $150.00, through Mr. C. Markoe, a merchant of this place. I do not need it and will not use it, though I am paying the expenses of Capt. Jim Ward back to the States. I found him out of money at Cordova, working hard and hopelessly, and anxious to go to his home, his mother and sisters. I knew how he felt, and placed my purse at his disposal. But just think of poor Ma, alone in that strange land, *waiting—just waiting.* I wonder often how she manages to pass the time. I know she must be unhappy; but I expect she has her Bible and her knitting. I know too that she must be suffering at this moment renewed anxiety at my long delay."

Passing over the beautiful description of his trip to Havana, which he reached on Feb. 11th, we will let him tell of the meeting with his mother. "After a short walk we reached Santa Isabel Hotel. I looked impatiently over the list of arrivals, and found that on the 17th of the month before was registered the name simply, 'Mrs. Slayback.' Asked if she was still there. 'Yes.' Sent up my card, and after waiting about twenty minutes in the parlor Ma came in, very little changed apparently in the five eventful years which *had changed me so much.* I felt that she had grown younger and I so much older. After the 'preliminary scene,' and all that, we had a conversation to the point. She urged me to go home. I did not wish to. She persisted that I must accompany her. I was induced to return with her, depending on the promise that you had made to me, that you and your child would return with me to my exile if I could not remain in that country." After a rough passage they reached New York Feb. 18th, where his mother parted from him, he going to Washington to receive a pardon from the government, and she returning to Missouri.

July 21, 1866, Colonel Slayback located in St. Louis, and renewed the practice of law. His success was grand and continued. He stood without a rival among the young lawyers of Missouri. The records of the various courts show that as a jury advocate he gained a larger and lost a smaller proportion of cases than any other active practitioner at the St. Louis Bar. Out of thirty-six cases in 1874, he appeared in twenty-five for defendant, gained nineteen, had

three hung juries, and lost only three. In eleven
he appeared for plaintiff, and gained all but one,
in which he was nonsuited. In 1873, out of more
than forty cases, he lost only one. His knowledge of human nature, joined to his delicate tact
and pleasing address, gave him thorough command in the examining and cross-examining of
witnesses. Persuasive and convincing, as an
orator before a jury he stood pre-eminent. A
contemporary says: " The style of his eloquence
is peculiar and characteristic : with earnest force
and persuasion he speaks to the heart and
feelings, as well as to the sober reason of his
hearers. When kindling with his subject, he
becomes animated and rapid, his illustrations
are most felicitous, and his logic thus embellished
rarely fails to please and convince. By intense
application to his studies in his profession, and
a varied miscellaneous reading, he has not lost
his fondness for the classics, but evinces in his
daily work the advantage which is ever to be
derived from the discipline their study gives."

Col. Slayback was throughout his life a consistent Democrat. No consideration of emolu-

ment could have swerved him from his principles.
Never a time server nor an office seeker, he
bore himself grandly before his fellow men without fear or reproach. He was a delegate from
the Second Congressional District of Missouri to
the Democratic Presidential Convention of 1876.
In the same year he was the Democratic nominee
of that district for Congress, but owing to an
unhappy division in the party a Republican was
elected over the two Democratic candidates.

Col. Slayback served two terms as first Vice-
President of the Bar Association of St. Louis, in
1879-80 and 1880-81. Twice he was chosen President of the Law Library Association by a large
majority. Of the second election he said : "At the
annual meeting of the St. Louis Law Library Association this evening I was elected President by
a vote of forty-two out of fifty-seven : there being
two or three other candidates in the field, this was
a very gratifying endorsement of my administration, during which I have introduced some radi-
cal changes in the management of the Law
Library (which now consists of over 9,500 vol-
umes), among which was closing the Library on

Sundays. I favored this because I thought working lawyers work enough on the six working days, and ought to rest on Sunday." He was a member of the University Club, the Merchants' Exchange, the Merchants' Benevolent Society, and of the Legion of Honor, No. 6. He was besides an honorary member of the Knights of St. Patrick, and also of the Elks Club. No man in St. Louis was more frequently called on for a speech on public occasions. But whether addressing a society, delivering a eulogy on the patriotic dead, standing before a school of young ladies inculcating the highest sentiments of true womanhood, presiding at a banquet, pleading with his countrymen in behalf of measures that would lead the nation on to prosperity, or standing before a jury to urge the cause of right, he was ever the noble man, distinguished for honesty of purpose, full of generous impulses, convincing and captivating.

It would be improper to omit in this brief sketch the most important index of a man's character—his faith in God. In the winter of 1881, Col. Slayback's only son, a child two years of age, was very sick for nine weeks. The illness of little Alonzo, together with the too rapid motion of his own heart, led him to serious reflection on the uncertainty of life, and the need of settling the question of the future on a basis that would impart peace to his soul; for he had been taught the Bible from his earliest childhood by his christian mother. He was familiar with the great doctrines of christianity, and was a firm believer in the atonement of our Lord Jesus Christ and of man's need of salvation. He had a high reverence for the religion of those who manifested faith in God. He detested shams and shows; and with his keen perceptive faculties, and rooted belief in the basal doctrines of the evangelical faith, he could readily detect departures from revealed truth. He knew error in whatever neological form it might present itself, and he would tear away its specious covering and expose its native monstrosity. True himself, he had no countenance for that which is false.

In June preceding his death, the question of preparation for the life to come fixed itself in his mind. He felt it to be of the greatest moment to him, liable as he believed himself to sudden death, and often he would speak of the matter to his christian wife. Sometimes in tones of thoughtful sadness he would say: "I have put off too long these great questions that should long ago have engaged my attention and been settled by me." Were these feelings a presentiment of his early death?

Often he and his wife would kneel together, when in the most humble and contrite manner he would confess his sins, and He who ever hears the cry of the longing soul sent comfort to his anxious spirit.

In August preceding his death, though assured by the physician that he did not suffer with any chronic trouble of the heart, but only needed rest, he visited Denver in quest of health, and to see his youngest brother, residing in that city. It was a pleasant sojourn to him. There he met relations and friends whom he had not seen for years—among them General Bela M. Hughes, his early friend and adviser.

Yet it seems that amid all the happiness and diversion that surrounded him his mind was occupied with thoughts of death.

Ascending the mountain one day with a friend he grew quite dizzy, and turning spoke of it to the gentleman beside him.

"Do not look back or below, but upward," said his friend, extending his hand to assist him. These words made a deep impression: "Not back or below, but upward."

On his return home he related this little incident to his wife, remarking: "I there saw and felt how sure and sweet it is to trust in the Savior who died for me."

Yet he recoiled from the approach of death. Full of life, surrounded by a happy household, consisting of his devoted wife and six loving children, with a wide circle of true and admiring friends, in the very prime of manhood, it was but natural he should cling to an existence, so radiant with hope, so blessed with rich promise.

On the day of his return from the West, he handed his wife this little poem (which he had clipped during his absence from a stray paper), remarking as he did so: "These lines are expressive of my feelings:"

A LITTLE WHILE.

A little while, and then the old, old story,
   Will be my answer to the fond word, Come ;
A little while, and I shall see the glory
   That clusters round the bright, eternal home.

A little while, if I have done my duty,
   The morn of life will break upon my sight;
A little while, and in fair robes of beauty
   I'll enter to that world of fadeless light.

A little while to dwell in pain and sorrow,
   And give to others as I would receive ;
And then the coming of the bright to-morrow
   With heavenly balm that will my soul relieve.

A little while to tread the paths of sadness,
   And bear the cross a loving Savior bore ;
A little while, and then the dawn of gladness
   Will waft the crown to me on Eden's shore.

A little while to feel the tear-drops falling
   O'er those we love, now silent in decay ;
A little while, and angel voices calling
   Will raise their dust to see the charms of day.

A little while to toil for wealth, ambition,
   And all the joys a life on earth can give ;
A little while, and then the soul's condition—
   Oh ! shall it be for death? in life to live?

A little while, and pangs of death will banish
  The name and riches we have gained on earth;
A little while, and pleasures all will vanish,
  Then we shall count them all of little worth.

A little while, and o'er the silent river
  The boatman pale will speed his phantom bark;
A little while, and then the great Life-Giver
  Will rend the veil of desolation dark.

A little while, and those in peaceful slumber
  Will hear the call to come and take the land;
A little while, and we may join the number
  Who by the throne of white forever stand.

A little while, and we may see the glory,
  The kingly grandeur of the One who died;
A little while to tell the old, old story,
  And then go home to Christ, the Crucified.

He was pleased to attend church if he expected to hear the simple gospel. He loved to listen to a sensible exposition of the scriptures. The Sunday after his return from Denver, in company with his wife he attended St. John's Methodist church, and listened to a sermon from the Rev. Dr. Tudor. The subject was the parable of the sower and the seed, Matt. xiii. The discourse greatly pleased and deeply affected him. Mrs.

Slayback, who had watched his development in
the christian life with the sincerest interest and
satisfaction, urged him to unite with some church,
assuring him she would go with him wherever he
might make choice. "We will join Mr. Robert's
church," he said—the Holy Communion (Epis-
copal). The Sunday previous to his death he
said to Mrs. S.: "Let us go to hear Mr. Robert
to-day. He is my old friend and is chaplain of
our Lodge." Mr. Robert preached from Joshua's
farewell to the Israelites. The sermon, which so
graphically portrayed the earnest spirit of the
departing leader, and so forcibly set before the
listeners the necessity of forsaking idols and
cleaving to the Lord our God, made a deep impression on the Colonel's mind; and that evening,
as he was leaving the house for a short time to
see a friend, he turned to his wife and said:
"Find that chapter for me, and put the book on
my study table. I wish to read it before I go to
bed. I have made idols of everything—my profession, my family, my learning, my ambition,
and I find them all as this"—striking the ashes
from the cigar he was smoking. On returning

he read the chapter, remarking, as he closed the Bible, "How beautiful!"

The next morning, as the husband and wife knelt together for the last time, he prayed earnestly for forgiveness. He was enabled to yield up all to Christ. Then he implored God's blessing on his children. Before leaving the room he said: "Do not correct the little ones; only pray with them."

The last week of his life was an unusually busy one, but he spent Wednesday evening with his family. Showing his books to some of the older children he remarked: "These will be a legacy to you, my children, from me." He idolized his children, especially his only boy, little Alonzo, the youngest.

Friday morning he descended to the breakfast room looking unusually well and happy.

The day was full of pressing demands. He kissed his wife "Good-bye," and mounted his noble steed, "Black Prince;" then turning in his saddle and waiving his hand to his little boy, Alonzo, saying, "Good-bye, my boy," he rode rapidly from the front gate down the street.

These were the last words from his lips to the ear of his loving wife and children. That night he was brought back to the bosom of that late happy household—dead. He had passed from earth at five o'clock October 13, 1882.

The stricken wife and children must ever bear in mind this memorable day, that robbed them of their protector and support, leaving them to mourn the loss for which there is no reparation.

The mother who nurtured his early years, and watched with grateful pride his development into a grand manhood, his two brothers, Charles E. Slayback, of St. Louis, and Preston Trabue Slayback, of Denver city, and his only sister, Minnie, the wife of Dr. Y. H. Bond, of St. Louis, all survive him.

He left six children; Susie, Minnette, Katie, Mabel, Grace and Alonzo.

His funeral was the largest ever known in St. Louis. The throngs that filled the old family mansion and crowded its grounds, and blocked the street as far as the eye could reach, composed of all nationalities and classes—ministers of the various denominations, judges, lawyers, artists, teachers, men of business, clerks, all professions and ranks—attested the high esteem in which our noble citizen was held. And the earnest look and tearful eye bespoke their love in language far more eloquent than the wealth of floral tribute that literally covered the casket where the dead friend lay, and sent from every part of the spacious parlors the silent incense of their sweet perfume.

For more than three hours an unbroken line of mourners filed past the bier, to gaze for the last time on the still form and pale face of him they had known and loved in life, and now sincerely mourned in death.

The body was escorted to its temporary resting-place in Bellefontaine, and afterward removed to Lexington, the home of his childhood. It now reposes in Macpelah cemetery, beside that of his father.

Juvenile Poems.

Public Speech.

When bold young men, of talents fair,
Their earliest public speech prepare,
They first attempt the frightful stage,
With " scarce expect one of my age : "
But I'll not tire you any more
With what you all have heard before.
Some two or three weeks since, my teacher
(Who surely is the queerest creature,)
Gave me a speech, with the condition
To learn it for the exhibition.
In all my life I ne'er had spoken,
And thought it really was provoking,
To speak the first time in my life
Before the public and his wife.

But now, as my great speech is over,
I trust, good people, you'll discover
That I'm a modest, youthful man.

1854—Masonic College, Lexington, Mo.

THE SNOW BATTLE.

The jeering taunts and bitter scorn
  Of fellow-soldiers sting his soul:
Friendless, despised, disdained, forlorn,
He had the taunt of "coward" worn,
Till, desperate in his shame, he'd sworn
The brand should from his brow be torn,
  Or death his daring purpose foil.

His heaving breast and flashing eye
  In vain with firmness meet the throng;
In vain does he the charge deny—
Vain by such means for him to try,
To prove the whole a slanderous lie,
Invented by some enemy,
  In mean, revengeful, causeless wrong.

Stern prejudice and public hate
  His broken spirit beareth down:

Excited passion's raging heat,
And all that slanders can create,
Or falsehood's fiction fabricate—
All, all, increase the crushing weight
  Of changing fortune's blasting frown.

But blissful hope soon cheered his heart—
  A bloody battle draweth near:
Valor and joy alternate start—
He longs to act the hero's part,
And by some act in warfare's art
Hurl back false slander's deadening dart,
  And prove his bosom knew no fear.

The puissant foe, in numbers great,
  O'erbalance freedom's feeble band;
And veterans in confused retreat,
Wheeling, recoil at rapid rate:
Too weak the thundering shock to meet,
They leave behind a brave defeat—
  But lo! where does the " coward " stand?

The battle's rage is blazing high,
  Death seals his victims all around;
The shrieking bullets shrilly fly,
The pealing cannon rend the sky:

Hundreds he sees around him die,
All wallowing in their blood they lie,
   Yet palls he not, nor yields his ground.

He stands when no one else dares stay—
   No friendly fellow now is nigh;
Their fleeting feet are far away,
Escaping death and fire-fierce fray;
Contented, when they'd lost the day,
To vow the enemy should pay
   A double price for victory.

But he, his holy honor lost,
   Felt 'twas not life to him to live;
He recked not, counted not the cost,
But faithfully maintained his post:
His single arm opposed the host,
Made many a foe yield up the ghost—
   Should death his character retrieve.

Like lightning 'long the line he flies,
   Gun after gun in arm he sets—
To cannon's tube the match he plies;
The volleys, sounding through the skies,

Are mingled with the dying cries
Of his advancing enemies,
   Charging with bristling bayonets.

They come in march by martial pride,
   Expecting many foes to find,
But find this one alone, astride
An empty cannon's brazen side:
Their whole detachment he defied—
Swore from the field he thus would ride,
   Or perish there and stay behind.

They paused—and, trembling 'neath his frown,
   Wrapt in mute admiration stood:
The men refuse to pull him down,
Or stain such bright, fair-won renown.
Although a foe, his brow they crown
With laurel, and in candor own
   His was a gallant soldier's blood.

They bore him through the martial crowd
   Upon his lofty soldier's car;
With heart-felt cheers, both long and loud,
His very foes his deed applaud,

As, whirling on his chariot proud,
He hastens to the free abode,
  A favored prisoner of war.

Exchanged, he homeward turned with speed,
  And to his comrades hastening sped ;
Long served his country at her need,
And, from the tongue of slander freed,
Enjoyed her freedom.   All agreed
Soldier ne'er boasted braver deed,
  None more nobly fought and bled.

LEXINGTON, Mo., Jan. 9, 1855.

IMPRESSIONS.

I saw a man, and liked him well—
His heart seemed full of generous blood,
And honor seemed his acts to impel ;
Thought I—" the image of his God."

I knew him better—and the more
I knew the more I found him vile ;
A hypocrite, who always wore,
O'er fiendish thoughts, an angel's smile.

(A smooth-faced hypocrite, who wore
A devil's heart and villain's smile.)

*　*　*　*　*　*　*　*

I saw a sweet and gentle fair,
At least 'twas so at first she seemed ;
Meekness seemed traced in every air,
And kindness from her bright eyes beamed.

I saw her oftener, and lo !
The illusion left my wondering eyes ;
Where smooth the words and sweet their flow,
Below a Tartar's temper lies.

I saw her more, and soon discover
Her sweets are but the arts of guile,
Assumed to please some brainless lover,
Who, fool-like, trusts a woman's smile.

"Tis thus where'er in life I go,
I find my first impressions wrong ;
The world is a deceitful show,
Women and men a lying throng.

A man is seldom what he seems,
A woman or an actress never;
Better acquaintance never deems
A man the better known, less clever.

1855.

VALENTINE—TO M. F. B.

Though I may wander far from thee,
   And long may not return,
My heart will but more faithful be,
   My love more brightly burn.
For thee—and only thee—my soul
   Breathes forth each gentler thought;
My heart, hopes, prospects, you control,
   Fair Mary, in thy heart.
But one bright image rules my heart,
   One smile alone I prize,
That smile thou only canst impart
   From thy seraphic eyes.
One cherished object only claims
   My homage and my love,
And 'neath her eyes' celestial beams
   My spirit's current moves.

Feb. 14, 1855.

Lines Written in an Album,

FOR LIZZIE COBB.

I write not, Lizzie, to invoke
On this remembering line
Thy criticism.   We o'erlook
All faults at friendship's shrine.

No languid lover's fainting sigh
Shall here disgust thine ear;
No words of genius meet thine eye,
But friendship most sincere.

" There is a friend," the wise man says,
" That sticketh closer than a brother;"
'Tis such a friend at present prays
Thou'lt be to him just such another.

He does not ask for worldly fame,
But begs for heart-felt friendship's blessing ;
Not friendship that is but a name,
But friendship worth a friend's possessing.

'Tis such that you are fit to give,
And bless some heart in that bestowing ;
'Tis such my youth would fain receive,
And strengthen in my older growing.

Here forced to mingle with a throng
To every feeling incongenial,
My life in anguish drags along,
And is, like theirs, severely menial.

Like every son of adverse fate,
I'm doomed to spend my days in sadness;
And yet, to shun my fellows' hate,
I'm forced to counterfeit a gladness.

Dec. 25, 1855.

To ——.

A bird may touch the earth,
An angel leave the sky,
A queen forget her lofty birth,
And love an humble eye.

Gems oft in mine are found,
Rare pearls hide 'neath the sea,
Bright sunbeams kiss the ugly ground,
Then why not you kiss me?

Lexington, 1855.

FORGET ME NOT.

When loving friends are loth to part,
And anguish sickens every thought,
This modest flower from heart to heart
Conveys a fond " Forget-me-not."

In terms as eloquent as tears
It asks what men have always sought,
In absence, distance, or long years,
The heart's last wish—" Forget-me-not."

And as we leave you, gentle friends,
If we may wish so dear a lot,
With this meek flower till memory ends,
We humbly ask, " Forget-me-not."

LEXINGTON, 1855.

TO MISS MARY WALTON.

When sweet, confiding friendship shows
A trust in one who feels forsaken,
The grateful heart forever flows
With gratitude time cannot weaken.

And when, fair lady, I return
Thy generous friendship's trusted token,
It is not strange this breast should burn
In gratitude more felt than spoken.

Receive again this emblem then
Of confidence, and trust the token ;
And take my pledge to be thy friend
Till life's last hour, unchanged, unshaken.

The slanderer's tongue, the whisperer's art,
Will ne'er a moment's doubt awaken ;
For faithful friendship from the heart,
When once bestowed, is ne'er retaken.

The wrongs thy sex has done this heart
Are henceforth, for thy sake, forgiven ;
For though some act a fiendish part,
Some act like angels sent from heaven.

An ardent soul forever chilled,
A faithful heart forever broken,
Till life's temptation's storm is stilled,
Will not forget thy soothing token.

Jan. 31, 1856.

To Miss Bella McC——d.

Unseen, yet loved,
Admired, and yet unknown;
That love approved
By thee, and thou alone
Shalt be beloved
As my unrivalled own.

Feb. 14, 1856.

To Fannie S.

[A Valentine.]

May not a modest little orb
  Sometimes draw near the sun,
And in its near approach absorb
  A splendor not its own?

'Tis thus thy smiles, like sunbeams bright,
  Light up my heart, when near,
With fancied rays of happy light
  From thy more brilliant sphere.

But now, the dear delusion past,
  I see in cold despair

49

The light I borrowed cannot last,
  Unless thy smile is near.

And since that smile can ne'er be mine,
  But must another bless,
I say farewell—yet, maid divine,
  I own I love no less.

Feb. 14, 1856.

Un Sequitur—To F.

Then be that friend
Till life shall end,
And these scenes have passed,
  Whose kindness and
  Affection blend
In union to the last.

  I cannot cast
  Thy image, fast
Engraven, from my heart:
  Though hope be past,
  The constant breast
Forbids love to depart.

I've said farewell,
I've tried to " quell
The impulse of my heart; "
But all too well
I love thee still—
Too late discerned thy art.

Though love is vain,
You shall remain
Unrivalled in this breast,
Till Death's dark reign
Shall banish pain,
And grant the spirit rest.

To F——.

You would like to see me in my shroud,
When cold death is on my brow,
When my prostrate form in the dust is bowed,
'Neath the conqueror's spareless blow.

You would like to see me in my shroud,
When by pain and death brought low
The warm soul is chilled, the heart once proud
Has forever ceased its flow.

And when crushed 'neath the king of terrors' tread
    Is the breast that once heaved high,
When Death has his icy fingers spread,
    And has dulled the flashing eye—

You would then stand by the dismal pall,
    And among the heartless crowd,
Who so oft the tear shed unfelt let fall.
    You would see me in my shroud.

When the gush of joy no longer flows
    From the fountains of the soul,
When the heart beats not, and no longer glows,
    But submits to death's control—

You would stand beside the unmourned bier,
    And behold its ghastly gloom;
And this form, bereft of its living fire,
    Wrapt in vestments of the tomb.

You would see the cheek like moveless stone,
    And the eye as dull as lead;
You would see the cage whence the bird had flown,
    The cold clay whence life had fled.

You would look upon the abandoned wreck,
    That is stripped of all its store,

When no hand, no power, its fate can check,
    Or recall it to the shore.

You would see the remnant of what once
    A devoted friend had proved;
Who had listened wrapt to the tender tones
    Of a voice too dearly loved.

You would see in the windings of the shroud
    A poor lifeless, rigid form,
That once spurned false pride, and never bowed
    In submission to a worm :

Who had loved to list in mute delight
    To the soul inspiring song ;
Or in sought seclusion spurned the sight
    Of an incongenial throng :

Who had loved the charm retirement lends
    To the soul that seeks repose;
Who was ever faithful to his friends,
    And forgiving to his foes :

Who was crushed at times with inward woe,
    And to misery consigned ;
Had learned to love what is most men's foe,
    A melancholy mind.

Then is this the wish thy heart responds
    To my soul's kind wish for thee ?
Has compassion then lost these soothing tones
    I had hoped encircled me?

Though it pains to think 'twas asked by you,
    Yet I hope 'twill be allowed ;
And since thus you wish, I will wish it too—
    May you see me in my shroud.

And though shocked and startled when I heard
    Such a wish, so strangely given,
I am grateful for the unstudied word—
    And may we meet in heaven.

Feb. 16, 1856.

To Tillie Russell.

The pleasing charm of young life's happy dream
    Sheds round thee its enchanting spell;
And lavished pleasures pour their golden stream,
    Each sigh, each sorrow, to dispel.

What wealth or smiling fortune can bestow,
    To sweeten life or banish gloom ;

What constant love of faithful friends can do,
   All join to bless thy youthful bloom.

Religion too, that hope which most we prize,
   With radiant beauty is combined;
And youth's pure incense floats up to the skies,
   An offering from a stainless mind.

What more can dearest friendship wish for thee?
   I'll wish your cheeks may know no tears;
And may your life, in future's doubtful day,
   Be always what it now appears.

Feb. 20, 1856.

To "Pleasant Retreat."

Can you tell why the eaglet abandons the height,
Where, above storms and dangers, rocks guard
   his young life,
And with pinion impetuous hastens his flight,
To engage in life's ceaseless and dubious strife?

Though his aerie is dear and its sunshine is bright,
Yet far from its scenes is the game he must seek;

And though genial the day, dark and dread is the
    night
Which englooms the abode on his stern natal peak.

Though it pains to depart, he cannot remain,
For activity urging impels him to roam ;
He must pass through the clouds as he spreads to
    the plain,
But they hide from his back glance the sight of
    his home.

Siren " echoes " from " fairy" inhabited " glens "
May allure, but they cannot induce him to stay ;
To Necessity's mandates and Nature's commands
Milder pleasures must yield—and he hastens away.

Can you tell why he wanders?   'Twere needless
    to ask ;
'Tis his destiny's call, and compliant he goes :
He has wings to be strengthened, then why should
    he bask
In the sunshine, in sluggish, inglorious repose?

St. Joe, May 24, 1856.

FROM ORLIE.

Had some one said, when first we came,
And were with trembling fondness pressed,
That time so soon could cool thy flame,
Then wildly raging in this breast—
I had smiled with contempt at a thought of change,
And, with vows of devotion forever,
Would have sworn most sincerely no power could
    estrange
My affections from Orlie—no never!

But brief have been the fleeting hours,
And swiftly, sadly, have they flown;
And, like the charms of withered flowers,
That youthful love is crushed and gone.
As the flame now obliterates every line
That was written so sweetly and fairly,
So the flame-like and withering breath of time
Has consumed my affection for Orlie.

My love was like this changing fire,
And blazed with momentary glow,

And was the soonest to expire
When most I thought the flame would grow ;
But instead of the paper that lights this flame,
'Twas my heart which that fire has consumed,
And the ashes remaining more desolate seem
In the furnace they lighted, then gloomed.

July 5, 1856.

THE RECOLLECTED IMAGE.

The smile which won my trusting heart
Thy flowing tears may wash away ;
Chill monster Death may mock thy art,
And turn thy brilliant eyes to clay.

Then think upon the mournful past,
And ponder well the present hour ;
Smiles will not Death postpone at last,
Appease his wrath, oppose his power.

Vain as the look you give your glass
Will all your love of conquest prove,
When Death his last decree shall pass,
And call you from your " work of love."

Ah! then remember in thy youth
That beauty's brightness must decay,
And seek those charms of sense and truth
Earth cannot give, nor take away.

No longer let thy pride of power
Provoke the vain desire of praise;
Turn from the follies of an hour,
To Heaven your aspirations raise.

That glass will in a few short years
Reflect back wrinkles to thy gaze,
And show the trace of grief and tears
Where, self admired, thy smile now plays.

St. Joseph, Mo., 1856.

THE NAMELESS—UNNAMED.

I cannot breathe her buried name,
In vain my utterance tries;
For hushed in self reproachful shame
The quivering accent dies,
And memory says "Be still!"

That name, alas! how have I striven
Forever to forget—*forget!*
To bury in oblivion—
But, ah! it haunts me yet,
And starts the silent tear.

Bound to my heart as with a chain,
It will not be forgot;
The fettered thought will *fast* remain,
But still—I speak it not:
I cannot breathe her name!

Oft in the silence of the night,
When light nor sound are near,
Her image floats before my sight,
Her voice rings in my ear,
And whispers "Name me not."

That name, regretted though it be,
Can wake no fondness now;
I sorrow not to think that she
Proves traitress to each vow,
But that she has a name.

I breathe no curse, I raise a prayer—
Heaven will decide her fate;

Another now believes her fair :
I cannot love, I cannot hate,
Nor speak her perjured name!

I wish a happy life to him
Who now expects to make his own
That name, than which none sweeter seem ;
And may he ne'er have cause to mourn,
Or blush with shame, with anguish groan,
Because of that dead name.

St. Joseph, Mo., August, 1856.

HATRED.

The narrow limits of expression fail me.
Oh! that I had new words! I then could tell
All that my soul intensely feels for thee.
Bah! No words are wanting when sincerity
Prompts the fond utterance of the lover's heart.
I do not trust; I cannot then respect you;
Your passion cannot move me till I do.
If there is one whose nature I despise
It is the maker of a reckless vow,
Who rashly swears allegiance to-day
And seeks a novel sovereign for to-morrow.

Of all deceits, inconstant love is worst,
Most base, detestable, and unexcused ;
It is the cause of more unhappiness
Than half the vices that degrade mankind.
The child of vice may often be reclaimed,
But loving woman, when she once has set
Her strong affections on a faithless man,
Will feel the sting within her blighted heart
Till disappointment is disarmed in death.
1856.

Man's Inconstancy.

Wild as the ocean when tossed by the storm,
And wild as the mountain crag's desolate form,
Are the fickle and whimsical notions of man.
Their pride and approval alike I disdain ;
Their love and their hatred, affection and scorn,
Are fleeting and changing as hues of the morn ;
As the waters of ocean, run high and sink low,
As they alter and roll, as they ebb and they flow ;
They but mimic the acts of the popular mind,
Undoing in rage what in prudence they bind.
1856.

FATE.

Why in depths of dark despairing
Should a soul of fire and daring
Sink beneath the wearing, tearing,
   Torture of a slow decay;
And, irresolute, surrender,
In a moment sad and tender,
All that years of tears could render
   Dearest to a child of clay?

Yet I feel my life declining,
And my chafing soul repining,
Clouds without a silver lining
   Bringing on the night too soon;
While the ghosts of midnight track me,
And malignantly attack me;
While my sun without, an acme,
   Sets and leaves behind no moon.

Thus to live unknown to glory,
And to die without a story,
Prematurely worn and hoary,
   Old in anguish—not in years,

Is the lot of millions, sleeping
In the doomed, repulsive keeping
Of oblivion, dread and sweeping,
　　As an ocean formed of tears.

Tears, vain tears; how unavailing
To sustain a spirit failing,
Emblems only of the quailing
　　That the proud heart loathes to feel:
Then let Fate her fierce darts shiver
'Gainst my soul—it shall not quiver;
Nay! the darkness of Death's river
　　Cannot fix an endless seal.

1856.

———

MOONLIGHT THOUGHTS.

A trembling moonlight bathes the hills,
　And tranquil is the air;
A calm serenity distils
　An incense sweet to prayer.

As on the shady wings of night
　Each moment floats away,

What heart beneath yon peaceful light
  Can bid one moment stay?

Or can man's power e'er check the flight
  Of moonbeams o'er the sea?
Or can the eye which sees yon light
  Resist its beauteous ray?

No more can heart restrain its love,
  When kindness, smooth as moonlit hills,
And gentle as affection's glow,
  Sheds its soft radiance on our ills.

St. Joseph, Oct., 1856.

[Written under a Cloud.]

FRIENDS! BAH!

The tear may start, the heart may ache,
To feel that friendship is a dream;
But ah! when trusted friends forsake,
The soul deceived recoils from them.

The earth knows not a friend sincere,
The tool most useful is best friend;

Of those we have the most to fear
Who most to friendship's ties pretend.

But still we foolishly believe,
Trusting, though finding all untrue;
We curse the old friends who deceive,
And seek the fickle smiles of new.

The tear may start, the heart may ache,
'Tis useless—men will still deceive;
Those most obliged will first forsake,
And deepest their rank venom leave.

St. Joseph, Oct. 15, 1856.

TÓ MY BOOKS.

When blind Fortune frowned,
  And destiny bound
My boyhood with fetters of want,
  My affections were turned
  From a world that I spurned,
To the wisdom your pages implant.

  Sweet soothers ye are
  Of my sorrow and care,

And relief to my aching heart bring,
To brighten each way,
That Hope can display,
And soften adversity's sting.

Ye bade me despise
The hypocrite's guise,
And tear off false dignity's mask,
With treasures refined,
To store up the mind,
And find true delight in the task.

St. Joseph, Dec., 1856.

CHOICE FOR LIFE.

It is not Beauty, full of angel smiles,
That e'er can tempt my steadfast heart to love;
Nor weak Affection, with its well meant wiles,
Nor Love as changeless as the constant dove.

'Tis not Devotion, breathing ceaseless prayer,
Nor sweet Repentance, bathed in teary showers;
Nor Intellect, embracing, like the air,
The mighty planet and the humblest flowers.

' Tis not a Voice whose rich, melodious tone
  Can cause the heart to swell with joy or woe,
Nor Splendor, circled with its gem-set zone,
  Nor Hearts of Pity, melting toward each foe.

None of these can e'er my love allure,
  I would a nobler, better object find;
Unbound and free, my heart must still endure,
  Until I meet with all of these combined.

St. Joe, April 14, 1857.

LINES:

Written after leaving an Exhibition at Presbyterian Church,
Jan. 23, 1857.

High Heaven! is this a christian land?
  Where men that God adore
Who formed them with His mighty hand,
  And lent the mind its power?

Then why did that irreverent throng,
  When in the temple pressed,
Their stay one moment not prolong,
  Until they could be blessed?

Christ's servant stood with hand upraised,
  But rude and unimpressed
They would not hear the prayer he raised,
  Unwilling to be blessed.

A pagan would have knelt in awe,
  His idol being addressed ;
They scorn God's grace and slight his law,
  Despising to be blessed.

Beware ! O slaves of gold, beware !
  Lest you incur God's frown,
And urge, too late, your idle prayer
  Up to his awe-wrapt throne.

Oh! if you can believe our world
  Unruled by God on high,
Let not your children too be hurled
  Where torments never die.

Then trample not religious truth
  Before their watchful eyes ;
Such acts far more corrupt our youth
  Than those the fiends devise.

A Tress of Hair.

[To Allie during Estrangement.]

A tress of ring-like dark-brown hair,
Cherished as all that's left of thee,
I hide more fondly than Corsair
Secretes his treasure by the sea.
Its place is whisperless and lone,
No eye but mine the relic sees;
I love it, for it is my own,
'Twas given me ere I failed to please.

'Twas given me by a gentle hand,
That locked in mine was ever warm;
Each finger was a magic wand,
Too well their witching touch could charm:
Still as I bend in lonely woe,
Where none my glistering eye can see,
A tear unmans me—be it so—
'Tis not the first I've shed for thee:

Communion lost and sundered far,
The world's wild madness fills my brain;
I watch the twinkling of the star
For some fond token, but in vain.

Silent as diamond's flash, its ray
Once seemed to dance through space, and rest
Bright on the keepsake, then away—
I shrieked! it seemed to pierce my breast.

'Twas only fancy's dark despair
Shrouding my heart.   I looked to see
The lock again.   It still was there—
Still beautiful, serene, unchanged—
Not unlike thee when last we met.
I hate to think of thee estranged;
I, though forgotten, can't forget
You loved me then—or said you did:
This clustering tress is token yet
Of how the changeable are changed,
While constant bosoms throb and fret
With one true thought, the rest deranged.

St. Joseph, 1857.

A Stormy Night in the Court House.

Loud blows the wind, and as it fiercely shrieks
My heart gives back its wailing; for each sigh,
Each sob, it utters finds an echo deep

Within my heart, which now is not less sad
Than the wild melody of this rude storm.
The rattling shutters but ejaculate
Expressions of the cruel shock without,
While the sepulchral echo from within,
Resounding through these halls in dismal woe,
And yet unheard by all save my lone ear,
Are but the symbols of those frequent ills,
Those keen distresses, whose lugubrious tale
Is only heard within the secret soul,
Where their sad echo left, they're hushed forever.
Now raging wild, now melting tenderly,
The notes of piteous woe, succeeding rapidly
To the harsh growling of the tempest's roar,
As if to make atonement for the ire
Its sweeping swell displayed.   'Tis thus in life,
The things befalling us oft seem endowed
With a self-soothing power, curing themselves.
There was a blast unsoftened, fiercely rude,
And now there's pleasure in its following strain.
'Tis thus in life we often find delight,
When naught but pain and sorrow were presaged.
Then pour, ye furious winds, with all your furious
      might,

Your streaming strength against this building huge,
And turn its empty chambers and its halls
Into an instrument on which you play,
Discoursing music of so rare a kind
That it will instruct as well as please the ear.

St. Joseph, Mo., May 13, 1857.

To Allie During Estrangement.

Has deepening twlight's dusky hue
No lone retreat for thought and you?
Tell me, is there some quiet spot
Where Orlie sighs that I am not?
Is your heart colder when, alone,
You think of one loved, lost, and gone?
When on the stars of night you gaze,
And think of me and other days?
No star that twinkles pale at night
But glimmers o'er my paler sight,
And in compassion's mood serene
I stray and stand where we have been.
Thy voice I fancy near me still,
But as I bend to catch its thrill

The phantom tone eludes the reach
Of strained attention's painful stretch,
And chilling shudders o'er me swim,
O'erwhelming e'en my flighty whim.
Oh! why will not an echo roll
From absent lips to cheer the soul?
Is all forgotten and ignored,
That love once gave, when love implored?
Deep night its realms of distant orbs
Arrays in anguish, that absorbs
The buoyant thoughts that boyhood blessed,
And manhood's sterner soul distressed.

St. Joseph, 1857.

The Old Grove.

(song).

'Tis sweet to think of those we love
  When they are far away,
But sweeter still that dear old grove
  Where we were used to play.
    The balmy breeze
    Swept through the trees,
    Lulling or soothing care;

And in that grove
Were smiles of love
We've never found elsewhere.

The cruel axe, with savage blow,
Has here and there destroyed
Some lofty tops, where last the glow
Of evening sunshine toyed.
The balmy breeze, etc., etc.

1857.

THE OLD OAK TREE.

To Edward T. Shields, of Jackson County, Mo.

Where Wea's humbled, withering race
Late kissed their conqueror's silver mace,
And dwell to imitate the ways
Of civilizing art,
Within the prairie's loneliness,
Hard by a tangled wilderness,
A tree in native loneliness,
There grows apart.

Not tall, but spreading far and wide,
With branches matched on every side,

Decked like a blooming forest bride,
      With gorgeous foliage ;
She stands in summer's sweet array,
And tempts the coolest breeze to stay
And kiss her ere it hastes away,
      To execute its embassage.

Beneath that tree's benignant shade
A band of weary travelers strayed,
And, ceasing from their labors, made
      A long sought resting place.
Blessed friendship sweetened their repose,
Around them bloomed the scented rose,
And not one thought of bitter woes
      Disturbed their quiet peace.

Their hearts were cheerful, brave and true,
And well meant wit responsive flew,
Congenial souls united grew,
      Beneath that noble tree.
Brave hearts need not the ties of blood
To join them in fond brotherhood,
A kindred link binds all the good
      In one great family.

Time scatters changes all around,
And sunders ties that love has bound;
Their foot-prints now are dimly found
    About that loved tree's base:
And still its drooping branches sigh
To every breeze that passes by,
Because they are no longer nigh
    With words of grateful praise.

But memory clings to that old tree,
Connecting it with joy and thee,
The souvenir let it ever be,
    Of friendship tried and true.
Remote be death's detested call,
Be time indulgent to us all,
And gently may its changes fall
    As Wea's summer dew.

Aug., 1857.

To Orlie.

I loved thee once, but now the flame
    Has perished like a blaze;

No more can Hope arouse the love
    I felt in other days.
The past seems covered with a veil,
    The future with a cloud;
And truth declares no heart can yield
    Devotion, and be proud.
Oh! love will be repressed by pride,
    And pride brooks not a frown;
Love floats not with so light a bark,
    But anger weights it down.
Repentance may desire again
    What love at first enjoyed;
But love can never flourish more
    Where it has been destroyed.
The heart is never offered up
    But once in sacrifice;
And if 'tis not accepted then,
    Its tone of fervor dies.
But if accepted with a smile,
    And then cast idly by,
Pride will not let the tender gift
    Slighted and bleeding lie.
But Pride the cherished offering takes
    In stern yet kindly care;

Pours soothing balm within each wound,
  And stays each springing tear.
Your kindness cannot please me now,
  I heed not now your praise;
No more can hope revive the love
  I felt in other days.

St. Joseph, Mo., Aug. 8, 1857.

WHO HAD THE BILL TO PAY?

Ah ! it was very nice indeed
  To travel through the State,
And visit friends who love to feed
  A friendly candidate :
How nice too did the lager beer
  Drink with them every day ;
But tell us, gentle Bobby dear,
  Who had the bill to pay?

Bob thinks the railroad through our State
  Will tell of him so well,
That 'twill his name perpetuate,
  When he beyond shall dwell :

Perhaps he built it, but we fear
   Posterity will say,
" Pray tell us, gentle Bobby dear,
   Who had the bill to pay ?"

Bob thought a seat in senate good,
   The pay was very fair ;
But still, he thought he rather would
   Prefer the Governor's chair:
But now, if in the doubtful race
   Sweet Bob has lost the day,
I wonder who in such a case
   Will have the bill to pay.

Aug. 14, 1857.

AN OLD TEACHER.

Year after year, with patient care,
My Cameron guided me to truth,
And taught me by his precepts rare
To curb the follies of my youth.

Profoundly skilled in buried lore,
And gifted with a taste refined,
'Twas his to point, mine to explore,
The pathway to improve the mind.

And now I see him leave his Greek,
And go to teaching whining girls
The proper way to smile and speak,
And show with grace their shining curls.

Aug. 15, 1857.

TO THE PREACHERS.

Written in an Album.

To the preachers and teachers your book is devoted,
That their names may here live when their deeds
 are forgot:
Asked, "What sort of a man by this name was
 denoted?"
You will say, " Ah! he lived, taught or preached,
 and is not."

Let the learned or the pious then write their names
 here,
But no pedant or hypocrite sully these pages ;
And may all most worthy your friendships appear,
When in judgment aroused from the slumbers of
 ages.

St. Joseph, 1857.

REFLECTIONS.

Written when about to leave the Court House.

Sadly, sadly now,
Burns the midnight light,
And my aching brow
Shudders at the sight.

Loudly, loudly, roar
Midnight breezes round,
But my soul no more
Saddens at the sound.

Swiftly, swiftly, life
Rushes to the tomb,
Through the lists of strife,
Through the halls of gloom.

Wildly, wildly, storms
Beat across my path;
Fearful in their forms,
Dreadful in their wrath.

Sternly, sternly, pride
Conquers every fear.

Fates! ye are defied!
Strike! ye Furies, here!

Vainly, vainly, fall
Strokes of bitter fate;
Earth has lost its gall,
Feeling left its seat.

Hours of woe may come,
And restore again
To their former home
Anguish, tears and pain.

Gladly, gladly, soul,
Take thy transient ease;
Soon the bell may toll,
Death may break thy peace.

Changes may await
That you little reck,
Sorrow weave a net
Slyly round thy neck.

But with changing life
Stop not to deplore;
Arm thee for the strife,
Sigh and pine no more.

Let each varied scene
Thou art doomed to pass
Make thee more serene,
And refine thy dross.

So thou yet may'st learn
To smile when some would weep,
Darts of fate to spurn,
Peace to nurse and keep.

St. Joseph, Mo., Oct., 1857.

WRITTEN WHEN A STRANGER.

Nobody cares for me,
    And I for nobody care;
We meet in the street,
    With a curious stare;
But no one will greet
    The stranger there;
Not even deceit
    Has a bow to spare;
Nor lowliness one conge.

Nobody smiles on me,
  And I on nobody smile;
Alone in a crowd
  Of both virtue and guile,
The high and the proud,
  The low and the vile,
Seem alike endowed
  With strangeness, while
I know not who they may be.

St. Joseph, 1857.

MISSOURI RIVER.

*Written while watching the waves from the stern of a
steamboat on the Missouri River.   1857.*

Foaming waters, madly leaping,
  Fling their waves upon the shore;
And they murmur, ever keeping
  Timely music in their roar:
And the tireless wheel is plying,
  Like the bounding pulse of life,
While, in distant calmness dying,
  Waves are melting from the strife.

Ceaseless streams of panting bubbles
Come escaping from the wheel,
Like the constant little troubles
Fate has destined life to feel;
While we watch their fretful races
Up and down upon the waves,
Others come to take their places,
And they sink into their graves.

So in life our fierce contentions
Into tumults oft arise,
While successive new dissensions
Chase the former from our eyes:
Gently smothered by the distance
Facts will lose their great intents;
Memory vainly makes resistance
To the current of events.

STRAYING THOUGHTS.

Oh! my thoughts are straying, straying,
Straying faster than the cobwebs
That are floating on the breezes,
Hazy breezes of the air:

For the winter is approaching,
And the changing hues of autumn,
Saddened by the chilling breezes,
Softened by the bluish hazes,
Fill the soul with vague and dreaming
Love for all the good and fair.
The sun appearing drowsy,
Shining like a sleeping beauty,
Tinges everything with mutable
And fleeting floods of beauty;
And the trees are gently sighing
O'er the ruin of their foliage,
Like a faded fair, lamenting
That her tresses, once so pretty,
So luxuriant, and so winning,
Are becoming gray and rusty.

St. Joseph, Nov., 1857.

LOVE.

Oh! love is madness—blind and rash and wild:
Stubborn as age, and foolish as a child.
It conquers sense,
And sways the heart;

Hates innocence,
          And studies art;
Destroys the object it at first adores—
Enjoys, abandons, and at last deplores.

'Tis said he holds the world in abject rule:
If so, the earth is monarched by a fool;
          For if we trust
              What we are told,
          Love turns to lust
              As it grows old—
Becomes as selfish as when young 'twas free:
Is such a monster clothed with purity?

Anger and hatred, love and pride and fear,
Are passions suited to the humble sphere
              Of fallen man's
              Degraded state,
          And no such plans
              To elevate
Our notions of our poor estate and birth
Can make a beast, born wingless, fly from earth.

It is the destiny of birds to soar on high;
Of men, to eat, think, talk, drink, walk and die.

What mockery then
It is to say
That mortal man
Can passion pay,
Of such a noble and unselfish kind
As ne'er was known, except in God's own mind.

St. Joseph, Dec. 1, 1857.

CHARITY.

Men love to magnify their own good deeds,
But still they listen when self-interest pleads.
The orphan's tear,
The orphan's cry,
They see and hear
Without a sigh,
Unless the piteous, painful tear and tone
Become by natural sympathy their own.

Instruction, impulse, springs to cure the wound
Of the poor wretch who weeds upon the ground.
Our frantic pride,
So stern and cold,

Is laid aside
When we behold
A sufferer unexpectedly disclose
A tale of sorrow, shadowing forth his woes.

But let the soul have time to think again
Of its dear self, its pleasure and its pain ;
And we forget
The other's pain,
Caress and pet
Ourselves again.
'Tis strange, with its great popularity,
This Charity should be a rarity.

A generous reputation once obtained,
Cost what it may, must ever be maintained.
A liberal man
Is called to give
The most he can
While he may live ;
And when he dies, the cries he has relieved
Revive again from men sincerely grieved.

St. Joseph, Dec. 1, 1857.

DEATH OF A LITTLE GIRL
ON A WINTER'S NIGHT.

The swinging signs are squeaking
  Down the dismal street,
And the midnight ghost is shrieking
  Through the rattling sleet;
Sleeping hearts are beating,
  Heeding not the storm,
While weeping eyes are meeting
  Round a little lifeless form.

They watched its little heaving
  Eke the dreary night,
Till they felt a faint misgiving,
  All might not be right.
Gently drawing nearer,
  Silent in their fear;
Each moment made her dearer,
  As her end seemed drawing near.

But dreary, dismal midnight
  Passed, and left them there,
Watching for the daylight,
  Watching in despair.

When the light returning
  Their feeble lamp was burning,
But the fire of life was gone.

A FALSE ONE.

False one, if I could only mourn
  For thee as for the dead,
My tears could be the better borne
  Than those which now are shed.

But still to know that still you live,
  And still to feel you gone,
Is like the sleepless throbs we give
  For sleep at sleepless dawn.

How have you sworn you would not wish
  Away from him you love
To live one hour; and yet—so 'tis—
  The serpent draws the dove.

An angel could not break the spell
  That demons, gazed at, weave,

Nor sorrows torture souls in hell
  More fiercely than I grieve.

Yet why lament a fallen tree,
  A blighted flower, or wall,
Since time will bring us soon to see
  The ruin of them all.

Thus perish joys most fairly bright,
  Thus fleet our cares away ;
Until resigned we greet the night
  With glad farewells to day.

1857.

SONG.

The dreams of my boyhood are over,
  Thine image is fading away ;
And fate has forever bereft me
  Of one who could never betray.
The madness with which I deplore thee,
  But adds to the sorrows I bear ;
And the sadness with which I deplore thee,
  Only serves to embitter despair.

Oh! say, can thy spirit draw near me,
    To receive the devotion I bring?
And wilt thou, invisible, hear me,
    Or breathe a response while I sing?
If thou wilt but whisper me softly
    Some word as a token from thee,
I'll cherish thy memory fondly,
    Till Death shall restore me to thee.

St. Joseph, Jan., 1858.

To Allie.

Tho' my fond expectations of joy I must sever,
    My visions of bliss can be never estranged,
For beauty, alas! is as charming as ever,
    And mad Cupid's winning temptation unchanged.

When the red tide of life shall turn cold in my heart,
    And death on my pale dewy brow shall abide,
Oh, say! will a tear of regret ever start
    To thine eye, as you think of the lover that died?

Will you think, with one sigh, of his name and his
    love,

The affection that prompted devotion to thee?
Or bury forever the scenes of the grove,
　When you heard the bird music of sunset with me?

Will you hush in the depths of the unfathomed heart
　The moonlight of love, and the hills of our stay?
Or sigh that the passion of youth may depart,
　As the moonlight succeeds the strong light of the
　　day?

And oh! will you whisper a prayer up to heaven,
　Imploring its mercy to smile on a fate
As dark as the storm by the mountain blast driven,
　And bitter as scorn in a man that we hate?

St. Joseph, 1858.

To A. W.

There's a tear hidden deep in the eye,
　There's a sigh buried deep in the breast;
But in secret concealment the former must lie,
　And the other be ever suppressed.

There's a woe we must suffer and brook,
　That is sacred to one single heart;

Yet the sufferer will never betray by a look
    The distress which he scorns to impart.

And he struggles and strives to conceal
    The destroying infection within;
Bitter smiles gaily cover the pain he must feel,
    But his spirit still smothers it in.

As a flower externally sound
    Gives no sign of its inward decay,
But still scatters its sweet-scented odor around,
    While the summer winds waft it away.

St. Joseph, 1858.

MEMORIES.

Lip answers lip in love;
    In friendship, hand to hand:
Affection fosters only face to face;
    Mind answers mind, and intellects expand:
Thought leaps to thought, as bolts electric move,
Scorning the span of intervening space,
Flash through dark clouds, and then unseen embrace.

So does it seem when here,
  In darkness and alone,
I think of one whom once I loved so well ;
  When fancy brings distinctly back the tone
That stirred within me, all my heart held dear,
And filled my being with a magic spell
Soft as the music of a silver bell :
Then do I think that she in some way hovers by,
  And still congenial understands my mood,
Guesses my wish and gives back sigh for sigh,
  Joins me in sorrow, laughs with me in glee,
Grasps at my arms, and cheers me on to good ;
Woman in form—with angel traits imbued.

But when the enchantment ends,
  My solitude returns—
A solitude that in the busy crowd
  Haunts me as well as where my taper burns
Lonely and dim ; and when my spirit bends
A glance within I almost shriek aloud :
Patience ! by suffering we grow strong and proud.

April, 1858.

REALITIES—SOBER REALITIES.

My soul is sad, for earth is but a scene
Of disappointed sorrow and chagrin:
Each way I look for comfort I behold
New plagues arise, and new distress unfold.
There was a time when upward to the skies
Ambition's fire impelled fond hope to rise.
Inflated hope, that conquered every fear,
Then promised fame and wealth and bright career,
Adorned the future with each jewel bright,
That fancy taught could give me true delight.
But life is rushing to the horrid tomb,
With every shadow, every dismal gloom,
As deeply clouded, and as full of pain,
As the dark moments that oppressed me then ;
And all the joys and hopes, I then believed
Ambition prompted, and my heart received,
Have one by one forsaken my cold breast,
And left a bosom careworn and depressed.
Life is too real, common place, and plain,
Too full of plans and petty aims of gain,
Too full of tests for crumbling ropes of sand,
Too full of spirits, struggling to command,

Too full of selfish ends on every side,
To foil high purpose and aspiring pride,
For every man who sighs in youth for fame,
To leave the world the record of his name.
Oblivion, dread oblivion, waits for all,
Pride's hopeless prison, fate's eternal thrall.
Yet oh! how bitter to repress each sigh,
That pleads for glory that never can die.
How sad the first conviction of the heart,
When life's experience bids young hope depart;
When we are taught no more to expect the joy
That charms the soul of the aspiring boy,
Life has no pleasure, pleasure no delight,
That can compensate young ambition's flight.
True, we are taught these lofty thoughts must turn,
But 'tis a lesson we are loath to learn.
Does nature's impulse then so vainly burn,
As to infuse a passion we should spurn,
Instilling lessons we would fain unlearn,
Point to a path that none can dare to explore
Without due sorrows and afflictions sore,
In which each robe by Nature's children worn
Is stained by weeds or by the bramble torn?

To wander gaily o'er the green hill's side,
Free as the wind that stirs the troubled tide,
Is better than o'er smoothest roads to ride,
With cruel Nature for a senseless guide.
1858.

To ——.

The chandeliers of porcelain and gold,
That fling their flood of purple glory down
Upon the wondrous beauty of thy head,
Impart no splendor not already thine;
And yet this magic light, that seems to close
About thee as if conscious of embrace,
Reveals a loveliness that dares the search.
The marble goddess in thy gallery,
The alabaster huntress in thy hall,
But prove thy fairness, fairer than the best
And purest models artists have combined;
And there is living beauty—theirs its type.
Thou hast grand instruments of music too,
That seem attuned to match thy matchless voice,
A voice whose simplest tone is sweeter than
The classic harmony of master hands.
1858.

To I. T——.

In reply to "Sweet Memories of Thee."

When sad thoughts are holding
  My heart in their sway,
And remembrance is unfolding
  Scenes of joy now passed away,
Mid the sweetest and the fairest
  Of all that is dear,
Thy voice is the rarest
  To soothe me and cheer.

It enters my chamber
  When I am alone,
Like memory's echo,
  In its soft silver tone;
And sweetly it thrills me,
  As it calms me to rest;
No frowning world chills me—
  Thoughts of thee make me blest.

When my fond heart is bounding
  In devotion to thee,
Oft light tongues are sounding
  Thy praises to me;

But oh! they describe thee
  Far less than thou art,
In sweetness and beauty.
  Enshrined in my heart.

When thy loved voice is singing
  Far away from mine ear,
And " sweet memory " is bringing
  Fond images near,
Then let me be near thee,
  Our souls miugling free,
Till time shall endear me,
  My angel, to thee.

St. Joseph, Aug. 19, 1858.

PASSION.

O, Passion ! ere Repentance knew
The pangs indulgence brought to view,
My bosom throbbed in fond delight
When Beauty's vision blessed my sight;
But now I've learned to look with terror,
For fear t'will lead me into error;

And when a winning smile I see,
I teach my feet to turn and flee,
Before contrition's poisoned dart
Can fix its venom in my heart.

ST. JOSEPH, Aug. 24, 1858.

To ——.

Imbued with charms by Beauty only given,
  And charms that Beauty's Queen could not decree;
The Power that formed thee looked around in
    Heaven—
  Beheld His favorite, and then modeled thee.

Thy wisdom, goodness, intellectual grace,
  Thy dazzling beauty and thy form divine,
Impart celestial splendor to thy face,
  Yet make thy face the least attraction thine.

Imagination is the charm of song,
  And songs of thee are mere detraction vain,
For real attributes to thee belong,
  Exceeding all in Fancy's fevered brain.

ST. JOSEPH, 1858.

To J——.

Time may teach me to forget thee;
    I wish it could :
In painful pleasure I regret thee.
    Repentance should
Ere this, in earnest, have beset thee,
    And made thee good.

St. Joseph, Sept. 1, 1858.

Discontent.

Silver hinges on the doors,
Velvet carpets on the floors,
Gilded framing in the halls,
And Rubens glowing on the walls ;
Horses, carriages and wine,
Costliest dress, and jewels fine,
All that the world regards with awe,
Illumed the mansion at Gildaw :
But all the chandeliers of Rome
Could not subdue the splendid gloom
That Fléta felt within her heart.
Looking at all this wealth of art,

She paused, and shuddered at her glass :
" Mistress of all," said she.   "Alas !
How hateful now is all this pelf;
I am not mistress of myself. "
And tears both hot and bitter fell
Upon a statue's pedestal—
Marble statue—rare and cold,
And worth its very weight in gold.

1859.

A VALENTINE FOR ALICE.

Thy heart, the home of truth and love,
  Thy bosom free from guile,
Thy face illumed from above,
  Thy sweet angelic smile,
Are dearer than the world to me,
  Or hope's ecstatic joys,
And bind my heart as true to thee
  As chains that Death employs.

St. Joseph, Mo., Feb. 14, 1859.

YOUR PICTURE.

The faulty image of thy charms,
  Imperfect though it be,
Could it but give thee to my arms,
  Or change itself to thee ;
Or could I in these colors trace
  Thy changing glance and smile,
That glance would every care erase,
  And every woe beguile.

Afar from me, beloved, caressed,
  In thy more happy lot,
This image is a token blest
  That I am not forgot.
And still I cling with ardent grasp
  To aught resembling thee ;
The little left to me I clasp—
  It shall not part from me.

And oft I think these pictured eyes
  Assume a living light;
Yet still the fleeting fancy dies—
  Thy absence is my night.
These eyes could weep when I have wept,
  Could sparkle when I smiled,

With sweet reproving gaze have kept
  My thoughts from running wild.
And if my conversation strayed
  Upon unpleasant ground,
How often would a gathering shade
  My rattling tongue confound.

*   *   *   *

But deep within my heart portrayed
  Thine image is engraved,
In fancy's purest hues arrayed,
  In seas of beauty bathed ;
And when temptation woos my heart
  Toward things you do not love,
One glance at this will make me start
  To see thy frown reprove.
And still thy gentleness and art
  My sweet reclaimers prove ;
Ah ! should that impulse fade away,
  Life has no vision left
That can restore the cherished rays
  Of which I'll be bereft.

St. Joseph, Feb. 14, 1859.

EXPECTATION.

There is a rapture in the spirit, with an inkling of
    despair,
When fond moments are approaching, and our
    hopes enkindle fear,
When the heart's sweet concord waketh to soft
    music from a dream,
And a note of harshness breaketh, like a loved one's
    painful dream.
There are times when expectation, as it vergeth
    toward relief,
Brings a tinge of blissful ecstasy, with vague and
    fitful grief ;
When we know not, and can tell not, what is strug-
    gling for control,
Yet we know a conflict rageth on the battlefield of
    soul.
When the blessedness of hoping is embittered by
    a sigh,
And the sickness of a hope deferred of luster robs
    the eye,
Oh ! the waking, and the breaking, and the near-
    ness of a joy,
Is more painful than endurance when a thousand
    ills annoy.

To Miss Anna Stebbs.

To cheer the sad,
To help the weak,
To make hearts glad,
To soothe the sick,
To woo the sinful from their way,
By good example's quiet ray,
And plant the proper impulse well
In youthful bosom's gentle swell,
Is doing good, far better than
The noisy pulpit's fruitless plan.

And oh! how sweet
It is to share
Companionship
With one so rare,
Whose constant thought, from morn till night,
Is giving other hearts delight;
While deep within the soul's hid dell
There slumbers not a selfish spell,
But joys resigned, and buried hopes,
Like children's graves upon the slope.

The grassy mead
That greets the eye,

May not impede
          The breeze-like sigh—
Yet she who can relinquish self,
And show no more than grass clad vale,
Griefs whispered not to passing gale,
Such souls their Maker's work adorn,
To nobleness and glory born.

          And nobler still,
          And dearer too,
          Who sheds good will
          Like evening dew,
And wisely speaks a fitting word,
When 'tis needed and best heard.
Think not a life thus fitly spent
E'er fails of heaven's reward when sent,
Compensatory gifts to shed
In blessings on Miss Anna's head.

June, 1859.

THE RESTLESS FOOT.

I am one of the " tribe of the restless foot,"
    That ever has sighed for repose ;

Yet clinging to hope for a promise of good,
  No actual rest my heart ever knows.
  My head, my hands and my feet have their woes,
  Their woes of unrest, and perpetual throes
  Of action and motion without any close,
Of turmoil and tempest and ceaseless pursuit.

Pursuit, and of what? Alas! could I tell,
  Far better and happier could I abide ;
But something is urging me on like a spell,
  And passion is goading, and so too is pride ;
  And yet when my judgment is called to decide
  What it is that impels me, or what will betide,
  Mute vacancy pauses, and nothing beside
Gives a watchword to soothe me or quell.

November, 1860.

THE RECORDING ANGEL.

High o'er the golden gates of heaven
An angel sits upon a throne of pearl,
To whom the gift of purity and power
Is delegated from the throne of God,
To purge the secrets of the darkest heart

That seeks to screen its sinful thought from sight;
And when from earth's dark grave-bespangled sod
The forms that Death has clasped are yielded free,
That angel scans the record which in life
Each pilgrim has in deeds historic stamped:
Each thought becomes an act! each wish a deed!
As lasting as the stroke of felon famed,
It is the heart that is dissected there—
And, written on a magic tablet plain,
The every thought is infinitely traced
In characters that only can be read
By this one Angel in all God's Domain.
There read, and passed upon, the soul is saved
Or hurled to Death eternal, but the germ
Of its destruction, or its bliss, is known
To none but God, the angel and itself!

Nov. 1860.

PAYING THE PREACHER.

Written and enclosed with checks for $10.00 each to Rev. E. S. Dulin and F. G. Fackler.

Every creed has agreed on one question at least,
    Though in forms they essentially differ;
Apostles and bishops, and parson and priest,

On this point do not vary a wafer :
From Paul to Pope Nino, from Calvin to Bates,
In unison Spurgeon and Beecher,
No matter how much they dispute about rates,
Don't object to our paying the preacher.

MR. FACKLER'S REPLY TO ABOVE.

"It may be true, as you have said,
That parsons, priests and prelates,
'Tho' differing greatly in their creed,
Agree about the rates :
Essential points they may divide,
And hold on high dispute ;
On minor matters they decide
To take a common chute.

But then do not forget, my friend,
That they stand not alone ;
Their principle may well defend
More interests than one :
There is a rule of recompense—
When lawyers all agree,
A client's guilt or innocence
Depends upon the fee."

Dec. 25th 1860.

On Hearing of Father Cary's Death.

These hills, where once the grass was green,
  Are bare beneath the dusty tread
Of crowds, who now profane the scene
  Of hopes by-gone, and friendships fled.
The sylvan bower, the peaceful shade,
  No longer smile when summer comes;
And where we once in quiet strayed
  The roaring wheel discordant hums.
When sunset, in its grander whims,
  Reminds me of the wasted day;
The tear that in the twlight swims
  Is not for *Time*, but heart's decay.
For those who once were part myself,
  United so were we in love,
No longer share with me the shelf
  'Neath trees that stood within the grove;
But one by one, like hopes unblest,
  Their souls' departure shocks my sense,
Till, like the Bard, I sigh for *rest*,
  And pray for wings to bear me hence.
Trees, flowers, the grass, and some who ranged
  These once fair hills with me are gone!

These ruined hills! I too am changed ;
  Their death is token of my own.
Green velvet mantle, lost and dead,
  Destroyed by the tumultuous crowd,
Is emblem fit of visions fled,
  And youth's grand aims, no longer proud.

St. Joseph, March 16, 1861.

.To Allie.

Truly fond, and fondly true,
  We have lived and loved for years ;
You for me, and I for you,
  Sharing smiles and sharing tears.

Guardian angel, charm of life,
  Gem of faithfulness and truth ;
Sole to soothe my bosom's strife,
  Sole beloved, my *Bride of youth.*

Bride of youth, and bride of age,
  Mother of my winning child ;
Blessings on thee, darling cage
  Of my fancies, dark and wild !

Calmed by thee, and soothed to rest,
  Bathe my temples with thy breath;
Press me as you always pressed,
  And forget me not in death.

When remembered by my love,
  Tho' the world heed not my end,
I will feel no envy move
  Me to sigh for fame or friend.

St. Joe, May 19, 1861.

Miscellaneous Poems.

A Captive Missourian's Sigh.

[Steamboat Augustus McDonald, Lexington Landing].

When twilight's cool shadows bedarken the wave
    That oft in my childhood enveloped my limbs,
They seem but the curtains of crape round the grave
    Where my hopes are all buried with memory's
        whims.

'Twas here I once dreamed that the air was so pure,
    And the soil was so sacred, that none dare invade;
But alas! on the spot where my youth was secure,
    The tools of a Tyrant their stronghold have made!

Alas! for my country, my peace and my pride,
    The land of my birth is all bleeding and torn;
And dark o'er the waters her children are tied,
    And chafe in captivity, sad and forlorn.

July 25, 1861.

A. JONES.

Prisoner of War, Lexington, Mo.

Our friend, A. JONES, well known to fame,
    Throughout the land and nation,
As one whose fame could always claim
    His neighbors' admiration,
Had heard it said, by some great man
    Of spotless reputation,
That Blair and Lincoln had a plan
    Of endless subjugation.

Supposing that a citizen
    Of his grade and pretensions
Would be the first to suffer, when
    This scheme acquired dimensions,
His clarion voice, throughout the land,
    Arose in thunder tones,
To let the folks all understand
    The stand of " Alfred Joues."

With tragic vigor he proclaimed
    His sentiments and speeches ;
Claib. Jackson must, he thought, be blamed
    For running off *sans breeches.*

Abe Lincoln did not suit his taste,
   Too shallow in dilution,
Because he thought he had disgraced
   Our sacred Constitution.

These speeches not unheeded fell
   On Alfred's auditories ;
But many men remembered well
   His sentimental stories :
So when the Yankees sent their troops
   To occupy Missouri,
Full many fancies pictured loops
   For " A. Jones " in their fury.

To end a tale, so long, so sad,
   Permit me, in conclusion,
To say A. Jones quite shortly had
   His share of war's delusion.
While wedging through a window,
   To make good his retreat,
He stuck fast as a cinder
   In a Nova Scotia grate.

So now this politician came
   To realize the fact,

That bayonets played a closer game
    Than oratory's tact:
He sits a prisoner, in suspense,
    To know his stay's duration;
And ponders, while he reads events,
    On A. Jones and the nation!

July 28, 1861.

STRAY THOUGHTS.

There's not one thought of all the train
That, countless, courses through my brain
    But bears some trace of thee;
And not one star that gleams above
That is not luminous of love
    Beyond life's billowy sea.

There's not a shadow o'er me falls
But Fate's dominion dark recalls,
    As clouds remind of storm;
And midnight gloom but tells my heart
What life is worth with thee apart,
    Thou priceless, beauteous form!

Our Flag.

Let our banner be borne on the breeze of the morn,
     'Tis as pure as the dew-drop be-gemming its crest;
The emblem of heroes—a nation just born,
     Of sons who can die, but cannot be oppressed.

When its colors are spread to the gaze of the brave,
     They hail it with pride and devotion untold;
With rapture they welcome the bloodiest grave,
     Ere their birthright of freedom be bartered or sold.

It has ne'er known dishonor, unstained by disgrace;
     'Tis the safeguard of Beauty, 'tis chivalry's shrine,
Encircled by soldiers, who rush to the place
     Where the chaplets of patriot laurels entwine.

Then bear it aloft o'er the Southerners' soil—
     Defiance it hurls in the teeth of its foes;
And trembling before it invaders recoil,
     For freemen defend it, while tyrants oppose.

Dec. 16, 1861.

To Allie.

In my gloom, dejected, sitting,
     War's grim phantoms hovering near;

Through my fancy, forms come flitting,
  Youth and hope had once held dear ;

There they come in crowded vista—
  Vanish hideous shapes before them—
Radiant as Apollo's sister,
  While a rainbow circles o'er them.

Every charm and sweet perfection
  Aids the fascinating spell ;
Memory wakes each fond reflection,
  And the bitter ones dispel.

One there is among the throng,
  See her! in her modest guise ;
How I feel her thrilling song,
  And the witchery of her eyes.

She, pre-eminent among them,
  Nearer, brighter than the rest,
Shuts the door of memory on them—
  Now she's to my bosom pressed.

Allie! blessing of my life,
  Vainly are we torn asunder ;
Pride of youth, my gentle wife,
  Guardian angel, I have found her.

Now imagination folds her
 Fondly, trembling on my breast;
Present, absent, still it holds her—
 Purest, brightest, dearest, best.

Hardships teach me but to prize her,
 Separations draw her near;
I shall seek to be no wiser—
 Let me know she holds me dear.

Jan. 25, 1862.

THE MISSOURI EXILE.

[SONG.]

Missouri! my native land, why mock thee with song?
The day of thy bondage is cruel and long;
Thy best blood in exile, brave, manly and strong,
Still loves thee, dies for thee, yet flies from thy throng.

Missouri! thy children reck not where they shed
The blood that must free them from tyranny's tread;
They perish far from thee, in battle, in toil,
But smiles close their eyelids—they die for thy soil.

Missouri land! we come again with banner and
 plume,

Come proudly to free thee from thraldom and gloom ;
Our bright steel shall flash forth the traitors' just
    doom,
And tyrants and tory consign to their tomb.
    1862.

SOLDIER'S LAMENT.

Bright eyes may shine for others,
    For me they cannot shine ;
And parents, sisters, brothers,
    Can never more be mine :
I only live to perish,
    In exile and in hate :
No softer dreams I cherish,
    My heart is steeled to fate.

And she, the idol, dearer
    Than every joy beside,
When fortune placed me near her
    In happiness and pride—
She too, alas ! forever
    Has faded from my sight,
And Fate herself can never
    Undo affection's blight.

Nov. 17, 1862.

LETTERS FROM HOME.

They tell me she is beautiful,
　　E'en more than in that hour
When first my poor heart trembled
　　As it felt that beauty's power.
"More beautiful than ever!"　Nell!
'Tis strange my heart should swell
　　With feelings, as I read these words,
That manhood cannot quell.
Why do they write an exile thus?
　　'Tis not for him to know
The pride and bliss of being loved
　　By one in beauty's glow.
And oh! that fate our destiny
　　Should link but to divide,
And sunder us so cruelly
　　When she was scarce a bride.
How to my very core of hearts
　　The words of cold praise fly:
"There is more bloom upon her cheek,
　　More sparkle in her eye."
I scarcely think it possible!
　　But language has no word

To tell the thrilling pulse these lines
    Within my bosom stirred.
Her eyes were always bright with love,
    And lightning nestled there,
That flashed into her lovely soul
    With wild electric glare ;
And when the flash was over,
    The darkness came again,
More desolate and dreary
    Than I e'er had known till then.
Life seemed a curse without her,
    And she at last was mine ;
My wretchedness was changed to bliss,
    Ecstatic and divine.
The rapture of our mutual love,
    The smiling fates adorn ;
Affection's pledge from heaven was sent—
    Our little girl was born.
I saw her eye, exulting, on
    The cherub creature bend ;
Her glance on me with dearest thought
    I have ever seemed to blend.
The mystic spell is broken—
    I am banished from her side ;

While waves and hills and dreary wilds
Our aching hearts divide :
And cruel war, and battle fierce,
And cannon's swelling roar,
Leave me to only dream and die
For the woman I adore.

Batesville, Ark., Nov. 17, 1862.

THE PAST.

There are faces we never forget,
There are shadows that never can fade,
There are visions that last when realities set
In the gloom of oblivion's shade.

Time's splendor is fleeting at best,
Its colors and baubles decay;
But the heart and its treasures are blest,
And repose only brightens their ray.

Then why should we sigh for the light
That lingers round greatness and pride?
Let us cherish the feelings that yield us delight,
And spurn every yearning aside.

There is nothing we mortals can own
    But fades when no longer we live;
Fate sits on a tottering throne,
    And Death will claim all she can give:

But blessings there are that survive
    Every dart that Destiny can cast;
Let Ambition and Avarice strive—
    While they vanish, Affection will last.

Dec. 21, 1862.

TO ALLIE.

On the verge of mighty ocean, I have gazed upon
    the deep,
I have watched the magic motion of the waves that
    never sleep;
And while sacred eve descended, o'er the earth and
    o'er the sea,
As the day and darkness blended, I was thinking,
    love, of thee.

Crested billows, soft and changing, chased each
    other from the shore,

And thus I felt my thoughts were ranging to the
    heart that I adore:
As soft words of love unspoken gently break upon
    thy ear,
These waves no murmuring betoken, till their rest-
    ing place is near.

On the mountain top reposing, in the night wind
    cool and chill,
Radiant stars, their light disclosing, hover o'er an
    exile still:
There is something in their beaming that now whis-
    pers "All is well,"
And, in spite of darker seeming, Love still weaves
    its magic spell.

Wandering thus, dejected, lonely, far away my foot-
    prints rest;
Hope still looks to thee, thee only, when my bosom
    is depressed:
Whether hill or vale I'm tracing, mountain top, or
    shelly shore,
Patiently my ills embracing, for the woman I adore.

Dec. 21, 1861.

THE SOLDIER'S DYING WHISPER.

Near where the battle raged fiercely and wild,
Wounded and dying, how calmly he smiled !
. Smoke of artillery tainted the gale,
Wreathing each feature that grows marble pale ;
Clasping her miniature close to his breast—
Death fastens rigid the fingers he pressed.
Hush !   Is it conscience he struggles to hide ?
Where were his thoughts drifting last when he died ?

Lift away the curtains that darken my soul ;
One dying moment let Beauty control !
Send me back the light that flashed from her eyes ;
Let it illumine my heart while it dies :
Softly, still softlier, fall on my ear
Strains of word music, that once were so dear.
Vain is thy mockery now, Earth and Pride !
Tell her I heard her voice last when I died.

Clinging to memory comes back the hour
When, in the moonlight, we stood in the bower,
Stood there to pledge, by the calm stars above,
That " time and change should not alter our love."

Well hath this vow been kept faithful and true,
" Never another love, not loving you ; "
Should that voice o'er my grave linger to chide,
Tell her I thought of her last when I died !

Tho' long a wanderer, sundered afar,
Far from my native land, off in the war,
'Twas for her child and her honor I fought,
Not fame or glory, so oft falsely bought ;
Wishes by millions my aching heart sends :
Is it a phantom that over me bends ?
Phantom or real, ah ! let it abide !
Tell her I prayed for her last when I died.

July 21, 1863.

SONG FOR THE " MISSOURI."

The Yankee lads and iron clads
  Are welcome now to try us ;
With shot and shell we'll greet them well,
  Before they shall go by us.
With our banner floating o'er us,
Let the foe but come before us ;
Every gun will swell the chorus—
  Bomb, bomb, bomb, bomb.

We all were tars before the war,
    And know a thing or two ;
Our leader is our sort of man,
    And we're a jolly crew.
While a man lives to defend her,
The " Missouri " still will send her
Answer to the word " surrender :"
    Bomb, bomb, bomb, bomb.

For Southern girls and Southern rights
    " Missouri " breasts the wave ;
Her noble name will yet give fame
    To Carter and Musgrave.
Always ready for the trial—
    When the Yankee pirates come,
They will soon find out the style
    Of our bomb, bomb, bomb, bomb.

Shreveport, March 29, 1864.

ROSY WINE.

To sit with one—and one alone—
And talk and read and onward speed,
While far from crowds, through broken clouds

The moonbeams fringe the mountain's brink,
Is wine, I think, for gods to drink,

Under this rosy, sparkling wine,
My soul and thine
Would feign entwine,
Till two are one and both divine.

Between us two the waters blue
Assume the hues of azure true,
And Heaven is vividly in view;
    And, *entre nous*, your wondrous eyes,
    To my surprise, awake my sighs,
    And trembling I'm in Paradise;
Yet, *entre nous*, it will not do,
My dear, for you to say " adieu,"
And tell me this is nothing new.
1864.

FAREWELL.

[Respectfully inscribed to my Cousin Lou M. McDowell, Ala.]

Farewell! to the pleasing sensations
    That pelting and praising invoke;
Farewell! to the partial relations,
    Whom not even my follies provoke;

Farewell! to the gems I discover,
    Long hid in an unexplored mine ;
Farewell! when the mid-day is over,
    To the sweet-scented breeze from the vine.

Farewell! to the halls of my kindred ;
    Farewell! to the scenes of repose ;
Farewell! to the shadowy clusters
    Of jasmine, verbena and rose ;
And when far from the spirits that love me
    I meet with the callous and strange,
At midnight, in secret, t'will move me
    To think that your love will not change.

Farewell! and if farewell forever,
    'Tis no vacant, unmeaning refrain ;
But it wings from the heart as we sever
    Mute wishes of meeting again.
Tho' the blood which our veins both inherit
    Be as noble as any on earth,
Let us claim to be kindred in spirit,
    And not merely kindred by birth.

May 31, 1864.

THE NEWS FROM HOME.

A man or two murdered, a name or two stained—
A mill struck by lightning, a roustabout brained—
A consolidation of corporate powers—
A party that lasted until the small hours—
A runaway team, a theatrical row—
A lot of low gossip too vile for a sow—
A list of the wicked condemned in the courts—
A tame summing up of the out-of-door sports—
A few of the loiterers loafing at springs—
And this is the news that the newspaper brings.
  1864.

PURIFICATION.

'Tis said that the Goddess of Beauty arose
  From the foam of the boisterous sea ;
And the muse of the South will rise from her woes,
  And grow beautiful when she is free.

'Tis the fierce heat of fire gives refinement of gold,
  And its dross is but parted, it is not destroyed ;
And fate will our future good Genius unfold,
  Untrammelled, unsullied, uncloyed.

Those only can speak to a suffering world
    Who have suffered themselves—then they speak
        to the heart:
We ask for no solace when joy is unfurled,
    We remember no lesson that pleasures impart.

Then blest Revolution! affliction of God!
    While thy cries brood desolate over the land,
Souls ne'er to be conquered kneel kissing the rod
    That is held by an Ever-wise Hand.

1864.

I SIGH FOR THEE.

[SONG].

With restless foot, I've wandered far,
And trod the weary paths of war;
I've tempted death for native shore,
And mingled in the battle's roar;
In danger struggled to appease
A restless heart averse to ease;
Yet danger's charm is lost to me,
And still I sigh—and sigh for thee.

'Mid lofty halls, at lowly door,
I've shared the fare of rich and poor;
Strange faces now look strange no more,
They look like those I've met before.
I've sought exciting scenes in vain,
And changing brings no change of pain ;
My chafing heart roams yet unfree—
A prisoner still—it sighs for thee.

The sleep that once brought rest at night
No longer soothes with soft delight ;
No calm repose for me by day
Can freshen now my life's decay ;
But doomed to be unsatisfied,
Appeals are vain to Hope or Pride ;
In Honor's wreath I only see
Fresh cause to sigh—and sigh for thee.

The loss of rapture in thine arms
Is brought to mind by beauty's charms;
But still no smile awakes a thought
So deep, so dear, as you have taught :

The crowd's gay mirth brings no delight,
And eyes look dim that once looked bright;
My spirit sickens at their glee,
And still I sigh—and sigh for thee.

March 30, 1864.

———

TO ALLIE.

The shutters rattle in the blast,
    And clouds obscure the moon;
The midnight is already past,
    And day will dawn too soon.

And we must part! how sad the thought,
    That hearts like ours must sever,
And lose the joy our meeting brought,
    In tears or parting ever.

So rare are hearts that truly love
    Permitted to unite;
Apollo should be bid by Jove
    Prolong their parting night.

But duty calls: I haste away,
    At dawn I lead my men;
But, dearest, think of me, and pray
    To meet me soon again.

Texas, March 8, 1865.

The Burial of Shelby's Flag.

A July sun, in torrid clime, gleamed on an exile band,

Who in suits of gray

Stood in mute array

On the banks of the Rio Grande.
They were dusty and faint with their long, drear ride,
And they paused when they came to the river side;

For its wavelets divide,

With their glowing tide,

Their own dear land of youth, hope, pride,
And comrades' graves, who IN VAIN had died,
From the stranger's home, in a land untried.

Above them waved the Confederate flag, with its
fatal cross of stars,

That had always been

In the battle's din

Like a pennon of potent Mars.
And there curved from the crest of their leader a
plume
That the brave had followed in joy and gloom,

That was ever in sight

In the hottest fight—

A flaunting dare for a soldier's tomb,
For the marksman's aim and the cannon's boom,
But it bore a charm from the hand of doom.

Forth stepped that leader then and said, to the
    faithful few around:
        "This tattered rag
        Is the only flag
That floats on Dixie ground;
And this plume that I tear from the hat I wear
Of all my spoils is my only share;
        And, brave men! I swear
        That no foe shall dare
To lay his hand on our standard there.
Its folds were braided by fingers fair,
'Tis the emblem now of their deep despair.

Its cause is lost. And the men it led on many a
    glorious field,
        In disputing the tread
        Of invaders dread,
Have been forced at last to yield.
But this banner and plume have not been to blame;
No exulting eye shall behold their shame;

And these relics so dear,
In the waters here,
Before we cross, shall burial claim :
And while yon mountains may bear name
They shall stand as monuments of our fame.

Tears stood in eyes that looked on death in every
awful form
Without dismay ;
But the scene that day
Was sublimer than mountain storm !
'Tis easy to touch the veteran's heart
With the finger of nature, but not of art,
While the noble of soul
Lose self control,
When called on with flag, home and country to part,
Base bosoms are ever too callous to start
With feelings that generous natures can smart.

They buried then that flag and plume in the river's
rushing tide,
Ere that gallant few
Of the tried and true
Had been scattered far and wide.

And that group of Missouri's valiant throng,
Who had fought for the weak against the strong—
Who had charged and bled
Where Shelby led—
Were the last who held above the wave
The glorious flag of the vanquished brave,
No more to rise from its watery grave!

PIEDRAS NEGRAS, on the Rio Grande, July 4th, 1865.

OUR INVADERS.

We have fought you all unfriended,
    For the world sustained your crime;
And the rights which we defended
    Met the scorn of every clime:
Still they're no less dear and holy,
    In the dungeon wearing chains,
Than they were when Southrons boldly
    Chased you from Manassa's plains.

Lips once proud bend meek and lowly,
    Kiss the hands that struck the blow,
And submit to terms unholy
    From the gloating, beastly foe;

But think not in exultation
  All are stricken with dismay—
Some still cherish indignation
  For a fiercer, bloodier fray.

When the many knelt, faint hearted,
  To receive the cell and chain,
Some with vows renewed departed
  From the accursed foe's domain;
And in patience we are waiting
  For the wrath of God on high,
'Gainst our stricken land abating,
  To avenge the outraged cry.

We are not the first example
  Of a nation crushed, oppressed;
Every race has records ample,
  Freedom's struggles to attest.
Oftentimes the blood and treason
  Seem expended all in vain;
But the avenger *Time* will measure
  All their outlay back again.

August 11, 1865.

To Allie.

I have no heart for study,
   And I have no heart for song;
The days seem everlasting,
   And the nights are just as long:
I have pondered over pages,
   'Till their faces are alike;
And I count the listless pulses
   Of the town clocks as they strike.
Now the watchman's lonely signal
   Shocks the stillness of the night.
And anon the stars I gaze on
   Pale before the coming light.
" All's well!" the town is sleeping,
   But there is no rest for me;
My soul is filled with weeping—
   In vain I seek repose on earth,
When absent, love, from thee.

August 13, 1865.

"Not for Me."

The stars are flaming out to-night,
   But not for me—but not for me;

Their sparkling beams are fraught with light,
    But not for me—but not for me;
Their radiance mocks the dismal gloom
    Within my heart—within my heart;
For every hope hath found a tomb
    Within my heart—within my heart.

Beyond yon mountain's towering crest
    I scan the sky—I scan the sky;
Each night renews my fruitless quest—
    I scan the sky—I scan the sky:
No ray among the millions there
    Will leave the rest—will leave the rest—
To soothe the darkness of despair
    That fills my breast—that fills my breast.

My eyes have seen earth's beauties shine
    In dazzling glee—in dazzling glee;
But of them all not one is mine,
    Not one for me—not one for me:
In exile, solitude and care,
    Before my prime—before my prime—
I've watched the wreck of every prayer,
    And bide my time—and bide my time.

Monterey, Mexico, August 21, 1865.

Home and Loved Ones.

I live but in the dreams of those
    Who once my pathway cheered,
Remembered joys, forgotten woes,
    And loves by grief endeared;
Youth's ecstasy and hope have fled,
    Its fresh and sparkling dew;
Its buds of promise, scorched and dead,
    Are lost forever too.

No longer throbs the bounding pulse
    Of boyhood's hallowed prime;
'Tis chilled beneath the world's repulse,
    By sorrow, not by time:
Misfortune and the frown of Fate,
    Like lightning's shivering spears,
Leaped startling through the storm of State,
    And buried all in tears.

Monterey, Mexico, September 10, 1865.

To the Belle of Missouri.

While forbidden to dwell 'neath the light of thine
    eyes,
    Or to breathe the sweet nectar thy presence dis-
    tils,

My absence and exile but teach me to prize
  The beauty that blooms on my own native hills.
Ah! sad were the moments when bidding adieu
  To a country oppressed by its bitterest foe;
With a tear o'er the graves of the faithful and true,
  And a curse on the dastard who shrank from the
    blow.

I have roamed into regions more genial and mild,
  And climates that glow with Italia's own blue;
But no beauty like thine on my vision has smiled,
  And no land has a daughter to rival with you:
In the blaze of their splendor, the wealthy and proud
  Have diamonds that flash with a ray from the
    skies;
But the jewels are vain as the forms they enshroud
  To out-dazzle the true sparkling light of thine eyes.

Sept. 26, 1865.—San Luis Potosi, Mexico.

To ——

From yonder antique dome the midnight bell
  Signals the watchman down the distant street;
Silence and vigil shed their mystic spell,
  Unbroken by the sound of passing feet.

Above Ayusco faintly beams the moon,
   The stars in all their glory mount the sky :
Around the eaves the gentle breezes moan
   With saddened sounds, that in the distance die.

At such an hour, the soul is all of fire,
   It seems absolved from contact with its clay,
And, like the light that glimmers from a pyre,
   Flies from its source, and wanders far away.

Ah ! there are feelings that the pen can paint,
   And others it cannot : the struggling heart
Breaks 'neath its burden, and all words seem faint
   To tell that story which none can impart.

What is the story ? 'Tis the secret tale
   That each life bears, with human shape endowed ;
The tale that makes the gambler's wife grow pale,
   Without a murmur—penitent, and yet proud.

It is the mother's anxious, smothered sigh,
   Over the errors of a sinful child ;
It is the calm of christians when they die,
   Or fierce remorse that groans in accents wild.

It is the patient absence of long years
   Between two hearts that mutually adore :

The exile's prayer—the agony and tears
    For one whose fate is hid 'neath ocean's roar.

        *   *   *   *   *

And here I pause—for I cannot express
    That which I wish to tell—to one? ay, two!
Wife of my youth, child of our tenderness,
    I have no world but you! Adieu, Adieu!
City of Mexico, December 30, 1865.

TO MY DAUGHTER SUSIE.

[Written in Mexico.]

To-day thy chronicle of life counts five!
    And he who should be near thee is away;
Thoughts leave my heart, as bees fly from a hive,
    To seek their favorite flower, its charms survey,
    And burdened with its sweets retrace their way.

Alas! poor child! God grant you ne'er may know
    The kindling fierceness of your father's heart,
Which makes him scorn to fear or brook a foe,
    Yet weep in secret from his child to part,
    And die of torture, ere confess its smart.

Thou dost not know me, pretty little one;
    You'd pass me by unknown upon the street:
Thy father's features, form, appearance, tone,
    Thy fancy doubtless paints, thy friends repeat—
    Yet ah! how sad the thought, we ne'er may meet!

Unknown to thee my yearning for thy weal,
    Unknown to thee my sorrow for thy woe;
Unknown to thee what pangs intense I feel,
    To think my only child—*a girl*—should go
    Upon life's path exposed to every blow.

Cruel the fate that severs me from thee,
    Susie, my darling; and more cruel still
That vain were my aims to make thee free
    From the despotic sway, and unjust will,
    Of foeman pledged to do thee every ill.

I fought to save thee! think of that, when blame
    Is muttered in thy presence 'gainst thy Sire!
Perhaps thy proud heart chafes in childish shame
    To hear the invader curse my vengeance dire;
    I hope again to make them feel my ire.

But all such thoughts are foreign to my theme.
    For every pulse beats gently at thy name;
I see thee nightly in my brightest dream,

And wonder if thy nature will be tame,
Or, like thy father's, glow with ardor's flame.

Ah! the rebuffs thy soul must meet on earth,
If you inherit but one-tenth my fire;
Perhaps you'll curse the hour that gave you birth,
And long for that which bids thy life expire;
I have oft done so in my phrensied ire.

DECKING SOUTHERN SOLDIERS' GRAVES.

"Pulveris tria maniplia ad manes Spargera."

Beautiful feet! with maidenly tread,
Offerings bring to the gallant dead;
Footsteps light press the sacred sod
Of souls untimely ascended to God:
Bring spring flowers! in fragrant perfume,
And offer sweet prayers for a merciful doom.

Beautiful hands! ye deck the graves
Above the dust of the Southern braves;
Here was extinguished their manly fire,
Rather than flinch from the Northman's ire:
Bring spring flowers! the laurel and rose,
And deck your defenders' place of repose.

Beautiful eyes ! the tears ye shed
Are brighter than diamonds to those who bled ;
Scorned is the cause they fell to save,
But " little they'll reck " if ye love their graves :
Bring spring flowers ! with tears and praise,
And chant o'er their tombs your grateful lays.

Beautiful lips ! ye tremble now—
Memory wakens the sleeping ones' vow ;
Mute are the lips, and faded the forms,
That never knelt down save to God and your charms :
Bring spring flowers ! all dewy with morn,
And think how they loved ye, whose graves ye adorn.

Beautiful hearts ! of matron and maid,
Faithful were ye when *Apostles* betrayed ;
Here are your loved and cherished ones laid.
Peace to their ashes ! The flowers ye strew
Are monuments worthy the faithful and true :
Bring spring flowers ! perfume the sod
With annual incense to Glory and God.

Beautiful tribute at valor's shrine,
The wreaths that fond ones lovingly twine ;
Let the whole world their ashes despise—

Those whom they cherished with heart, hand and
    eyes,
Will bring spring flowers ! and bow the head,
And pray for the noble Confederate dead !

May 9th, 1866—On Steamer Stonewall, Mississippi River.

To Jefferson Davis in Prison.

Dark, dark is the cell where thy foemen entomb thee,
   But, like the great pictures that mellow by time,
The anger vindictive which seeks to consume thee
   Will brighten thy virtues, but darken their crime !

Then prostrate defender of all that was holy,
   And sacred, and dear to the hearts that were thine,
By cruelty greatness was never made lowly,
   But grandeur in fetters is ever sublime !

Could hearts linked in liberty's hopeless endeavor
   Thine agony, pale and emaciate, atone,
They'd share it—and never forget it—ah ! never !
   Thy fault was thy people's ; thy greatness, thine
     own !

Then while Garibaldi and Kossuth are dining,
  No longer called foes when they once are o'er-
    thrown,
The American champion of freedom is pining,
  In a dungeon to suffer and perish alone.

Aye ! suffer and perish, for daily and nightly
  No moment of rest his torments allow;
The sentinels' tramp, and they do not tramp lightly,
  Is waking, remorselessly waking, him now.

The wife who so nobly has guarded his honor
  Is suffered at last to behold that dear face;
But the eye of a base menial slave is upon her,
  To chill back her tears by his impudent gaze.

Ah ! tell me of barbarous nations no longer,
  When torture exquisite as this is devised,
To wreak the unsparing revenge of the stronger,
  On one who though captive cannot be despised.

Then shackle with chains the wrecked form of the
    leader,
  Who marshalled his cohorts and fronted your line ;
The chivalrous, lofty and daring " seceder "
  Will soon be a martyr, heroic, divine.

Then murder by inches the soldier who fought you,
  Transmit to your children the damnable stain ;
And centuries hence, when the world has forgot you,
  'Twill honor the hero who now wears the chain.

June, 1866—Written on Steamer Kate Kinney, Missouri River.

CONTRASTS IN CITY LIFE.

Out of the sound of the voices,
  Away from the noisy street,
Where the reveller drinks and rejoices,
  And the sidewalks bruise my feet,
I am waiting the car to bear me
  To the city's outskirts grey,
Where my wife is waiting to hear me
  Recount the toilsome day.

I left her soon this morning,
  And little *Susie* asleep ;
All night we had watched the darling,
  Such watch as parents keep,
O'er her feverish, childish prattle,
  Our weary eyelids bent,
Till the fever ceased its battle,
  As the dawn with darkness blent.

Then with heavy heart I started
  To earn their daily bread ;
And I've toiled all day sore-hearted
  With the fear our child is dead :
Though none in the shop were braver
  To do the tiresome task—
The hour ! ah, for the favor !
  But 'twould cost my place to ask.

Now the car is moving slowly,
  Filled with hearts that do not think
Of the trials of the lowly,
  Who from their glances shrink :
I'll take my seat by a banker,
  Who has gained enough to-day
To store it away to canker—
  What ! could she ? and I away ?

The street cars thunder and rattle,
  The lamp jets fleck the street,
But silent now is the prattle
  That the father longs to greet :
He finds them alone in the cottage,
  The mother and pale dead child,
With no one to heed her sorrow,
  Or to hear her sobbings wild.

They both then bend their gazing
  On the smile-set marble face,
Till the taper ceases its blazing,
  And darkness drapes the place;
But while their hearts are bleeding,
  In squalor, dark and drear,
The banker's guests are leading
  The dance in his mansion near.

October 7th, 1866.

OUR DEAD.

Wake not the slumbers of the brave,
  Who for their honor fell ;
But let each everlasting grave
  Its mute suggestion tell.

They passed away in brighter days,
  In glory and in fight;
Ere valiant deeds had lost their praise,
  Or wrong subdued the right.

The hearts once lit with freedom's flame,
  That in the valley lie,

Now sleep beyond the reach of shame—
  We for the living sigh.

Hearts that indignant scorned to live
  Submissive to a wrong,
Had prized no boon that life could give,
  Or had not prized it long.

1866.

STERLING PRICE.

A MISSOURI POEM BY A NATIVE MISSOURIAN.

Written in 1866.

Dedicated to those whose generosity to the people of the South
would relieve the distress occasioned by war.

There was a time when anxious quest arose,
  To find a leader for a nobler band
Than Sparta's bravest. Fierce dissension grows
  From trifling matters o'er a stricken land,
When words political result in blows,
  And light dispute to deadliest hate is fanned ;
But Envy shudders when the times demand
A chief resolved against all odds to stand.

Men stood appalled! They had but heard of war,
  When brutal Hessians shot some hapless girls
And harmless men. Camp Jackson's lightning jar
  Down Walnut Street its bolt magnetic hurls.
St. Louis trembles! Passion, near and far,
  Contagion spreads. Civil commotion whirls
All systems into chaos. German churls
With Yankee fiends unite. The tragic curtain furls.

And what a scene! Arrayed on Freedom's side,
  Ready to strike for God and native shore,
After the boasting ranters all subside,
  There are some thousands who resolve to pour
Their last heart-drops of blood into the tide,
  Or win redress for wrong in battle's roar:
Patrician offspring offer there their gore,
If need be, to sustain the South's devour.

And yet Missouri did not seek their fight,
  In all the tumult she had plead for peace:
Doomed to be robbed, no matter who was right,
  The meek lamb's innocence saves not its fleece.
Both parties covet, and they both invite;
  We shun them both, and each cries "treason this!"
We lacked the sterner manhood of old Greece,
Or we had armed, and bid the quarrel cease.

We could have said, " We'll not invade the South,"
  Our property, like theirs, is menaced too ;
Nor will we rush into the cannon's mouth,
  Because John Brown was hung, as was his due."
Bad farmers cut their crop up in a drouth,
  Neglecting thus the little they might do ;
And so when faction rules, it will subdue
The little sense that might have struggled through.

No choice was left except to choose our side—
  Missouri argued for the Union still ;
A call for troops aroused her latent pride—
  For troops to carry out a despot's will—
For troops to scatter vengeance far and wide—
  For troops 'neath flags of "union" and "good-will ;"
To crush our brother, and his blood to spill,
That abolition rage might drink its fill.

This " call " was scorned by other States than ours,
  But " loyalty " was never questioned there ;
In vain Democracy opposed the powers
  The " Free States President " assumed to bear.
Old sailors wait not till the storm cloud lowers
  To trim their sails. States of the Northwest swear
" 'Tis wrong," "they won't," and, like a yielding fair,
They curse New England, yet her lewdness share.

The time for calm discussion is not yet,
    But men will wonder in the time to come
How strife could fling its drapery of jet
    O'er every door where Courage has a home,
By such transcendant bosh as Seward set
    To woo his trudging minions from their loam,
And place them following the fife and drum,
With deeds of brutal wrong that struck men dumb.

For twenty years the North had nursed its rage,
    For thirty years had threatened to divide;
" Part slave, part free," it was their motto sage,
    " This country cannot be : " so they decide
To blot their own slaves from historic page,
    By selling those they had, before they tried
Emancipation.   Then, 'tis not denied,
'Twas Northern men said, " Let the Union slide."

They took good care to sell their negroes first,
    Before they found out slavery was a sin;
They pocketed the cash with pious thirst—
    To soothe their consciences they squeezed *the tin*.
I never heard of Yankee yet who durst
    Not keep the price the Southerners paid in
For these same woolly-heads, who've been
The real cause of all this war-like din.

The sale completed, why should they ask more?
    They had the money, and we kept the slaves;
Our land and cotton added to their store,
    But Beecher, Greeley, Helper, Lincoln, Graves,
And many others of their kith and yore,
    Preached madness, till the truth itself depraves
The public heart, and red-tongued ruin raves
Over the wilderness of white men's graves.

Such was the national disease when we
    First realized the awful cry of blood;
And as each branch pines with its parent tree,
    Missouri's hopes are blighted in the bud.
The only question with us now must be,
    Where shall we find a man to stem this flood,
Who loves the Union, yet who has withstood
The meanness of this Abolition blood?

There were but two whose names both friend and foe
    Acknowledged overbalanced all compeers;
Both gained renown in wars with Mexico,
    And had worn civic wreaths in later years.
Poor John T. Hughes made graphic pages glow
    With tributes to the one, until he heard
His name a household word. He now appears
Unworthy mention in heroic verse.

The other was preferred, tho' many thought
    He was too calm amidst the storm of State;
A few malignants whispered, " he was bought,"
    Others asserted " he came out too late ;"
But faction, at his name, no longer sought
    To offer opposite a chief so great
Any less noted man as candidate—
All murmuring approbation left, the rest to Fate.

And soon—too soon ! their choice was put to test
    Upon the hard-won ridge called Bloody Hill;
Seven desperate charges for its gory crest
    Stained every inch of soil : the conflict still
Unchecked in fury, when that leader pressed
    On in the front rank—on, and on—until
A shout burst forth, so wild and deep and shrill—
The foe fled from him when they failed to kill.

No triumph ancient Rome allowed to those
    Who conquered Romans, for they could discern
No ground for glory in their country's woes;
    But when their land by civil strife was torn,
The victor and the vanquished at its close
    Mingled their ashes in one common urn ;
And shall our dear Missouri then be shorn
Of those illustrious wreaths her Price has worn ?

Oak-hill and Dry-wood, Lexington, Elkhorn,
　　Beheld his valor, strategy and zeal;
His counsels sage, **unheeded by Van Dorn,**
　　Of fatal sequence to Missouri's weal.
With fresher bays than all his brow adorn;
　　Though wounded, he made no complaint, appeal,
Or criticism.　He appeared to feel
All of his people's wrongs, yet he was mute as steel.

When he did speak, 'twas always of good cheer,
　　To rouse some faint one, or the strong to nerve;
His lips ne'er uttered where a man could hear
　　One word desponding, or whose tone might swerve
The wavering from their duty.　Rumors drear
　　He treated with contempt, as they deserve;
But when good news came, he would make it serve
To arouse the soldiers, and his hopes preserve.

From Boston Mountains, through the Cypress slough,
　　His troops through storm, thirst, heat and cold he
Defied the climate, and abandoned too　　　　　[led;
　　The land to ravishment for which they bled.
Ah! cruel trial of the soldier true,
　　To hear his wife and children cry for bread,
And yet his march resume with sickening dread,
For brutal Curtis stays to burn their shed.

What influence was it of the loftier kind
    Induced the brave, thus wronged, to be controlled ?
Was it alone the mastery of mind,
    Or genius dominant o'er common mould ?
No ! 'twas their leader's excellence, combined
    With " *Amor patriæ*," pure, unbought, unsold :
For Freedom's sake, thus freeman dare to hold
Their scorn for tyrants—their contempt for gold.

With these, obedient to his country's call,
    Our gallant chief for other scenes prepares ;
In vain the brave in hosts at Shiloh fall,
    New hosts supply the force their death impairs.
Missouri bleeds—forsaken, left by all—
    Her sons go freely where the bravest dares ;
And Farmington, Iuka, Corinth—bears
The world's stern history a tale like theirs ?

'Tis no part of my purpose to detail
    The varied exploits of our chief's career.
They were so numerous that prose would fail,
    And verse much more inadequate appear.
Missourians death-dealing forts assail,
    Missourians when *he* led them knew no fear ;
By foeman dreaded and by friends held dear,
His name was ever welcomed with a cheer.

Who led the van?   Who held the slow retreat,
    With stubborn rage, disputing for the ground?
Who killed the picket—marched the midnight beat,
    When lonely vigil starts at every sound?
'Twas those who followed him with sorrowing feet
    From far Missouri—land of home, and bound
By ties more dear than Tennessean mound,
Where many a green grave has since then been found.

Next followed scenes of warfare's grandest scale,
    Gigantic armies under leaders grand—
Names at whose mention myriad foes turned pale,
    Names that gave dignity to Freedom's band.
Could Beauregard, Bragg, Hardee, Van Dorn fail
    To win their knightly laurels in command?
Or Bowen, Marmaduke, Polk, Forrest, and
The other champions of the Southern land?

Armstrong and Chalmers, Breckenridge and Green,
    Cheyburn and Maury, Villipigue and Scott,
Shelby and Morgan, Parsons, Little, Stein?
    And thousands destined to obscurer lot
By war's stern fortune, yet who might have been
    Fame's chosen few—born ne'er to be forgot:
Emmet McDonald was, for instance, not
Less glorious that he fell in youth without a blot.

Corinth and Tupelo! trivial places once,
    Till rendered classic by war's tragic strife,
With clanging sabre, and deep booming guns'
    Re-echo daily.   While the drum and fife,
Drill and instruction, change the rustic dunce
    From citizen to soldier, till his life,
Devoted once to farm, home, babes and wife,
Was thus prepared for scenes of conflict rife.

'Twas there in muster, skirmish and retreat,
    The camp's routine soon practical became ;
The midnight vigil and the sentry's beat
    Seem more endurable, and far less tame
When lurking rifles watch the slightest cheat ;
    As hunters, when they seek for dangerous game,
Are cautious, yet alert.   Besides, there came
Immense reviews to fan the martial flame.

I saw a man among the titled great,
    With something more than mortal on his brow ;
Grandeur was stamped there by the hand of Fate,
    With modest dignity that could not bow,
Nor amidst adversity grow elate.   [endow
    When Fortune smiled! Does gracious Heaven
Man with His image?   Then behold it now ;
That face blends all that gods to men allow.

All eyes turned on him.   Men of higher rank,
  Yet less renown, appear to court his eye ;
Their courtesy recognized, he seems to thank
  His soldiers for that homage chieftains vie
One with the other to extend.   He drank
  No praises for himself.   Though proud and high,
Among the great he made no soldier shy
To approach the man whose word could bid them die.

Courtly of presence, yet the private's friend,
  He signed no warrant for a culprit's blood.
Anxious the line that loved him to defend,
  Reckless of danger to himself he rode ;
And never was his tall form seen to bend
  When smoky battle bathed him with its blood ;
But merging from its sulphurous clouds, he stood
Sublimely calm, defiant, unsubdued.

No act of cruel bloodshed stains his life,
  Pardon and pity fill his manly breast;
A hero in the battle-field's red strife,
  His captured foe became at once his guest ;
And he would bare his bosom to the knife
  Before the weak, by stronger, be oppressed ;
Friend to the sick, the wounded, the distressed,
To woman courteous, and by women blessed.

Magnanimous he ever was to foes—
    He gave back gallant Mulligan his sword;
And when the latter, like a soldier, chose
    Captivity, in place of honor blurred
(Refusing a parole), the wife arose,
    And asked to share the destiny of her lord;
Tho' troublesome the wish which she implored,
'Twas granted instantly—the only guard, their word.

The soldiers' idol, and the people's friend,
    Office-fed factionists detest his name;
No place so high, applause will not offend,
    When it gives promise of a lasting flame.
The great Epaminondas was condemned
    By envious rivals to disgrace and shame;
The names have perished that procured him blame,
His shines unscorched by Time's all-withering flame.

The less have ruled the greater many a time,
    As history of politics and wars both show;
Places are purchased; "luck" and sometimes crime
    Win high success, Macbeth-like, by a blow.
The first men of an empire seldom climb
    Into the ruler's office. They forego
Ambition that must rule or ruin—so
If self be uppermost, they care not who's below.

Vox populi, some ancient wise men thought,
  Should be consulted by shrewd "powers that be ; "
Perhaps if this old rule had been well taught,
  The British Tories would have saved their tea.
But sound experience always must be bought,
  And roundly paid for, or we should not see
The very blunders of last century
Repeated, to our cost, in '63.

Men often seek for places, but sometimes
  The place calls loudly for some fitting man ;
And this *vox populi* absurdly chimes
  Clamorous approval of the latter plan.
Wood, Lovell, Pemberton and Father Grimes ;
  No ! Mother Holmes I mean, and others can
(I beg old Grimes' pardon) prove the ban
Of putting pigmies out beyond their span.

Leaders are oftener wrong than those they lead ;
  Their followers see when they have missed the way,
Avoid the sloughs and quicksands that impede,
  And pass the paths that led the first astray.
Nations are happy when their rulers heed
  The ruder wisdom of the race they sway ;
Vox populi and common sense dismay
The pets, who spoil—and traitors who betray.

The times are passed that drew these comments forth,
    Great men for errors great atonement pay ;
The crushing columns of the mighty North
    Have swept the rulers and the ruled away.
For their success, perhaps their navy's worth
    Did more than fault of him who, doomed to pay,
The scapegoat of our failure, claims to-day
Our tears, to illumine his prison's gloomy ray.

The West, neglected, called its hero home,
    And he was sent as grudging gifts are cast ;
Jealous instructions, such as ruined Rome,
    Fettered his genius and his plans harassed ;
Yet he was welcomed as the ocean foam
    Thunders its greeting to Borean blast :
The golden time for his return had passed,
But patriots joyed to see his face at last.

The army rallied round their favorite chief,
    Discouraged skulkers sought the ranks again ;
A force was gathered in a period brief,
    By far too large for Holmes' contracted brain.
'Tis said a lady added to his grief—
    Her hand, with Helena, he might attain.
For thy sake, cruel Love, were never slain
Victims more noble than bedecked that plain.

Remonstrance was fruitless.   It was urged
    That such a force as ours could now invade
The unwalled towns and fields by foemen scourged,
    Redeem our State, and gladden every maid
Whose absent lover had thus far emerged
    Unscathed from danger.   But who can persuade
Against the homage to fair woman paid,
Whose bright eyes madden most just as they fade ?

We plead in vain.   And added to the shock
    Of our defeat and Vicksburg's stubborn fall,
We lost the valley—gave up Little Rock—
    Desertion hovered o'er us as a pall.
Like men condemned to die upon the block
    Our troops retired, deep gloom pervading all ;
Nor did they rouse till Shelby's bugle call,
At Arkadelphia, rang through camp and hall.

Still clogged by weakness in superior rank,
    Of many a fault our hero stood the excuse ;
Some pious people wondered if he drank,
    Some called his discipline severe—some loose ;
Some criticised the front and some the flank,
    But were apologetic in abuse ;
At last they cursed Head-Quarters like the deuce,
And wished "Old Pap" would carry out his views.

The struggle for Red River next began,
　With Commissary Banks and Steel combined;
One in the North, a formidable man—
　A formidable boast, the other signed.
But Richard Taylor rather spoiled the plan,
　On all sides, for before K. Smith could find
An equilibrium suited to his mind,
He had Banks whipped and scattered to the wind.

I envy not the laurels any wear,
　All that I merit are already mine;
But I despise a military air,
　And certain "stuck-up" ways hard to define,
Yet easy to be felt—and hard to bear.
　Lieutenants and drum majors of the line
Assume becomingly this sort of shine,
But *generals*—when plainest are most fine.

Hence, West Point etiquette, West Point red tape,
　And all that sort, are well enough in place,
But cannot make a soldier of an ape—
　The best trained mule makes but a shabby race.
Not all are mourners who display their crape;
　Church members are not always sure of grace;
A dwarf can never wield a giant's mace;
Cadet to general, is not mere gilt lace.

Price laid the plan to capture Steel complete,
   And had not interference balked his aim
No Jenkins Ferry had contrived to cheat
   The victor of his spoils.   But it did seem
A little too provoking that a fleet
   Should vanish slowly, like dissolving steam,
While the same meddling that broke Taylor's dream
Should shelter hopeless Steel from Price's scheme.

But, like a gamester who has saved a part
   Out of the fortune that he might have won,
A victory of deliverance soothes the heart,
   Tho' Shreveport wept for many a dear pale son.
From robbed plantations, homes and cities start
   The baffled foe's red flames, and columns dun
Shed conflagration's ruin o'er helpless one,
While Yankee ravage puts to blush the Hun.

Heroic Allen !   Governor indeed !
   Louisiana claims thy exiled bones !
Forever foremost at the time of need,
   Thy stirring voice was heard in thrilling tones.
No knight more courtly ever mounted steed,
   No chevalier a purer record owns ;
Thy gen'rous hand sooth'd orphans' sighs and groans,
Now e'en the stranger thy hard fate bemoans.

But why enumerate the fatal list,
    That soon or late fell at our hero's side?
To many a veteran eye 'twould bring the mist
    To tell how Weightman, Rives, Greene, Erwin died;
Or Churchill, Clarke (the boy artillerist),
    Slack, Porter, Kirtley, Farrington, McBride,
And many a mother's darling, father's pride,
That charged where Gates or Cockrell desperate ride.

My lay would have no end, if I should pause
    To name them all, for naming would be naught
Unless I gave my reasons for applause.
    They followed Price, and if that name is fraught
With fame, their merit was in part the cause.
    With them he counselled—under him they fought.
If pupils of his camp were not well taught,
Why was that madcap Shelby never caught?

Shelby! ideal of the modern knight,
    Who took a gun boat with his " horse marines! "
Most daring of the brave in stubborn fight,
    Who traversed mountains, valleys, swamp, ravines,
King of two rivers—Arkansas and White—
    His name revives the Revolution's scenes:
If means were wanting, he invented means,
Capturing his outfits—even to canteens.

The Southwest quiet, we again aspired
    To wrest Missouri from the Eagle's beak :
This dream Missourians' heart forever fired ;
    No soldier was too sick—no horse too weak
For marching when this darling hope inspired.
    It made a paradise of mountain bleak,
Made very heroes of the mild and meek,
And brought a livelier flush to every cheek.

Advance guard of the moment, thus designed,
    The restless Shelby seeks his old domain ;
Leaving the crushed and pent-up foe behind,
    On Croly's Ridge, he checked his war steed's rein—
Captured some forts, as if to employ his mind,
    While Price was coming with a heavier train ;
And proved in deeds, as few will prove again,
The vast resources of his fertile brain.

His bread on boards, his meat on sticks, was cooked,
    No tent or baggage his light troops impede ;
He struck the unwary foe when least they looked,
    With few encountered many by his speed ;
No long delay his fiery nature brooked,
    No fare effeminate his followers need ;
Their jest was danger, and their pride the steed,
" Old Joe " their idol—his commands their creed.

The devious windings of this long, last march,
   'Twould take some ingenuity to trace ;
The storm clouds chill us, and the sunbeams parch,
   Nights of unrest to dangerous days give place :
The attack, the pursuit, the capture and the search—
   The scout, the headlong charge, the picket chase—
The quick surprise, the old familiar face—
Sometimes a battle—and sometimes a race.

And there were scenes affecting in their way—
   Our people's joy was every where intense ;
Some long had waited to behold that day,
   Who hailed our flag as their deliverance.
Wives greeted husbands who could only stay
   To kiss their darlings lingering at the fence ;
And dashing off a tear, as they rode thence,
Invoked God's guardian hand in their defence.

Sometimes, alas ! what anguish greets the brave !
   Zealous to realize long-hoped delight,
And clasp the loved ones he had fought to save,
   As he drew near his homestead's cherished site,
Finds ashes, chimneys—and perhaps a grave.
   Revenge is wrong ; but so it is to fight.
The law of human nature makes it right—
Sweet to the smiter is the chance to smite.

If some took desperate reckoning for such acts,
    It was their only pathway to redress :
To those who knew the aggravating facts,
    Always concealed by mercenary press,
It was no wonder that the Federals' track
    Miss Anderson's avenger should harass :
Quantrell and Todd could scarcely have done less—
The very tiger heeds its cubs' distress.

                              [spared,
Sometimes they struck when soldiers would have
    But they no soldiers' quarter were allowed ;
No Mameluke or Tartar would have dared
    Their Ishmaelite defiance, fierce and proud :
Their lives were those of men who had despaired,
    Stung mad their breasts with morbid passions
Each belt with eight revolvers was prepared- [crowd,
Alike the informer, spy and red-leg fared.

I do not justify their lawless course—
    They sought no sympathy, and little felt ;
Their citadel, the brush ; their steed, their force ;
    Keen eye, their guard ; their arsenal, their belt ;
But still their deeds atrocious had their source
    In wrongs more savage than of Dane or Celt ;
Before Nemesis in their vows they knelt,
And outraged woman urged the blows they dealt.

Such outlaws Righteous Judgment ever sends,
    As Heaven's peculiar curse on civil war.
Let condemnation rest on who offends,
    Not one of these had followed Price afar :
If by his presence they conserved their ends,
    'Twas not his fault, and should not dim his star.
Their violence no rule but one could bar—
Each band's own chief was sovereign as a Czar.

We give back those who love us not their hate,
    The veriest cur is fierce when turned at bay ;
The power to conquer does not indicate
    The right to trample, or the right to slay.
Despairing cowards will assassinate ;
    But things of courage, hopeless of fair play,
Will turn like Sampson driven to dismay,
And perish frenzied—flinging life away.

Once more we left Missouri to her fate—
    Baffled by numbers, all our toil was vain ;
Once more our weakness drove us from the State,
    Too long resigned to hostile bayonets' reign.
There was no record of our triumphs great,
    A servile press insulted e'en the slain ;
But deeds of gallantry on many a plain
Atoned our sole defeat and soothed our pain.

Hail, Kansas! State of congregated thieves!
  We took one blow at thee in passing by;
Thy "loyalty" for "martyred" murderers grieves,
  And John Brown's ghost is worshiped with a sigh.
Jayhawking robbers of Missouri beeves,
  Thy Senatorial honors bear on high;
"Treason" in cloth of widow's loom ye spy;
In aught worth carrying off, "conspiracy!"

Our march was called a failure and a "raid,"
  Head-quarters met our hero with a frown—
Ignored the unselfish greatness he displayed,
  And sought to pluck the chaplets from his crown.
In vain attempts to censure him were made
  With footmen faint, who rode his chestnut brown,
When he to rest them on their way got down,
And walked to make the soldier's fare his own.

Deep indignation sided with our chief.
  He asked investigation. But why trace
The sickening sequel? 'Twould renew our grief;
  To Lee's surrender lesser woes gave place.
The struggle had been long—the close was brief;
  He sought, first, clemency for his lost race,
And then toward foreign land he sets his face,
And chooses exile rather than disgrace.

Thou who could'st bid thy marksmen spare a foe,
  Because he rode out boldly and alone !
Thou who a captured million didst bestow
  Back to its vault, the Bank of Lexington !
It wrings our hearts to think of thee in woe,
  Old, and impoverished, 'neath a foreign sun.
The brave forgive the brave. What thou hast done
America will claim. Then claim thine own !

Come back ! to those who yearn to take thy hand,
  Let our entreaties thy resolves entice ;
Come to thy cherished friends, and native land—
  A good example is the best advice.
A born commander can obey commands ;
  Opposing chiefs have urged thy pardon twice ;
Thy very foes have termed thee " free from vice "—
" Pure but mistaken patriot "—Sterling Price !

I write for Southern people. But, perhaps,
  Some one with candor left to hear both sides,
Who did not sympathize with our collapse,
  And feels no pity now, what ill betides,
Will read this story of disjointed scraps,
  And think its measures mere poetic strides.
The author to the future faith confides ;
The truth of all things time at last decides.

The great will live, no matter who defames,
   As mighty structures rise above earth's slime;
And when the day comes to recount proud names,
   Renowned for virtue in an age of crime,
And free from passion men discuss the claims
   That made " almost a nation " sound sublime,
Then those who love Missouri, in that time
Will see preserved true memories in their rhyme.

My strong hand trembles as I seize the pen,
   And feel it all inadequate to show
The glories of those great and gifted men,
   Whose names so feebly in these measures glow.
Let each who knew them pay his tribute then,
   And genius will in proper time bestow
Some writer, like the bards of long ago,
With power to tell well for us what we know.

Ah! how I covet this condensive power,
   This gift conferred by Nature on so few!
That I might rescue from oblivion's tower,
   And hold the virtues forth in living hue,
Of those we loved, but lost in luckless hour!
   Names of illustrious dead, whose names imbue
Their age with chivalry—imparting too
Renown to those who such a race subdue.

Fond memory lingers, wishing all undone
   That gives our country glory at such cost—
Gives back the weeping mother her dear son,
   And mourning maid the lover she has lost.
But God, who orders all things from his throne,
   Gives us the harvest—but he sends the frost;
Even His chosen, for wise ends He crossed,
And He chastises where He loves the most.

No triumph ancient Rome allowed to those
   Who conquered Romans, for they could discern
No ground for glory in their country's woes;
   But when their land by civil strife was torn,
The victor and the vanquished at its close
   Mingled their ashes in one common urn;
And shall our dear Missouri then be shorn
Of those illustrious wreaths her Price has worn?

Those times are past. But ere I close this page,
   One word to those who have this story read:
I write not in resentment, but to assuage
   Our captive grief for joys forever fled.
This sacred privilege should not enrage
   Our recent foemen. They but mourn their dead.
Much more we suffer; but when both have bled,
Mutual forgiveness mutual peace must shed.

Then let Americans implore High Heaven
  To look in mercy on our stricken land ;
Let good men bind where wicked men have riven,
  And learn a lesson from affliction's hand.
Forgiving, as they wish to be forgiven,
  May party spirit flee from Freedom's band,
And yielding homage unto God's command,
United millions round one altar stand.

THE UNION SOLDIER.

[Respectfully dedicated to Gen. F. P. Blair.]

He fought, as he supposed, to save
  The Union and its cause,
And struck to liberate the slave
  Against oppressive laws ;
But when he saw the slave he freed
  Turn on his prostrate owner—
A pinioned captive—'twas a deed
  That shocked a soldier's honor.

The breast he bared to battle's frown
  Sought none but standing foes ;

And when his enemy was down,
   His strife was at its close.
Oppression's foe is always brave,
   In triumph or disaster;
His mission is to free the slave,
   Not crush the prostrate master.

1867.

"UMBRÆ NOCTIS."

Night was not meant alone for those
Who, lulled in sleep, forget their woes;
But hearts that glow with hidden fire,
To solitude and shade retire,
To mock repose with smothered sighs,
While slumber waits on drowsy eyes,
Where hopeless shrines in secret rise,
To expiate unuttered cries,
That, checked through all the crowded day,
At last to agony give way.

Blest night! when hid from curious gaze,
Love's fervid flame may leap and blaze;
And flowers that far away have bloomed
Still soothe the soul to torture doomed.

When reckless of perdition's brink,
Within themselves the feelings sink—
When every sense grows faint and dim,
And sorrow's cup o'erflows its brim,
Till lost to all, but those bright eyes
That peer like stars 'twixt clouded skies,
One blissful phantom fills the sight,
That smiles—then flies—and all is night.

Ah! woman! woman! false or true,
The manliest brain thou dost subdue;
And quiet vengeance clothes thy form
With deeper dread than battle's storm.
The man who injures thy repose,
In vain would laugh away his woes;
In vain, midst gay companions, tries
To drown remorse with revelries.
Fly to distraction as he will,
Thy pallid face pursues him still;
And every pang he caused thy breast
Will rob his bosom of its rest—
Till joyless, phrensied and undone,
Nemesis haunts him when alone;
And when with others he is gay,
His callous air will still betray

Some lingering torture of regret,
He never—never—can forget.

The recreant wife, or truant maid,
That he has sought for and betrayed,
May think that she alone endures
Grief that repentance never cures ;
But ah ! the wretch who wrought the crime,
And scorned compunction for a time,
Will some day die—for die he must—
And then, for every forfeit trust,
Around his dying couch will stand,
With pointing finger, icy hand,
Each form whose innocence he wronged ;
And Retribution, though prolonged,
Will visit round his sabled hearse,
The echo of their ghostly curse !

St. Louis, Feb. 13, 1867.

GOOD IN SEEMING EVIL.

Troy fell, and her fugitives fled from her flames,
And founded an empire that conquered the world ;
And vanquished Jerusalem homage still claims,
Wherever a civilized flag is unfurled.

Leonidas died with his brave Spartan band,
  But Freedom survived her best children's defeat;
And he who at Waterloo lost his command,
  Through exile and death made his triumph com-
    plete.

Then weep not for those who for Liberty fell,
  Resisting oppression too cruel to name;
They share not a bondage too loathsome too tell—
  The glory is theirs—they know not our shame.

To Our Southern Belles.

Though the gems from your caskets, so ruthlessly
    torn
By the belles of the North, may be trophied and
    worn;
Yet the jewels they took were not jewels we prize,
For their splendor remains in the flash of your eyes.

Though your fathers' plantations lie barren and
    black,
Yet your riches remain—all the riches we seek;
For your smiles of appoval a dowry impart,
In the far vaster wealth of a welcoming heart.

Tho' insults and wrong plunged your households in
    gloom—
Past the blows that we struck to avert such a doom—
Yet we read a reproof for dejection and sighs
In the trust in to-morrow that leaps from your eyes.

Tho' the cause that we pledged in our vows to defend,
And the banners we bore, in submission must bend;
Yet forgive us our sin, if our woe we forget
In your smiles of "well-done" and "there's hope
    even yet."

Tho' now we've no coachman to send with our note
(For the North has found need for his wisdom and
    vote),
Yet the fellow who bears it I reckon will do,
As he serves me quite well since he left off the blue.

Brave girls of the South—brightest gems of the
    earth—
To a cowardly race you can never give birth ;
And 'tis you that as Liberty's altar expires,
Like the vestals of old, will rekindle its fires.

Since we fought for our honor, and not for applause,
Tho' vanquished, we cling to the wreck of our laws ;
And like Spartans will utter no cry of distress,
Nor a word of contrition our sealed lips express.

St. Louis, 1867.

CONSOLATION.

No flower to dewy morn awakes
   But some rude hand will pluck the gem,
Regardless of the wreck it makes
   Around the ruined stem.

So beauty, love, and all we prize,
   Some tempter hastens to destroy;
So Satan entered Paradise,
   When all seemed peace and joy.

So eyes that win, and lips that smile,
   Are those that soonest will betray ;
Like serpent glances, that beguile,
   Then seize upon their prey.

When thus from earth's attractions driven,
  The soul is taught deception's smart,
Faith whispers " there's a love in Heaven
  That satisfies the heart."

EPITAPH TO BE PLACED ON MY TOMB.

Let him who looks upon this spot
Remember soon 'twill be his lot,
And judge with gentleness, if he
Would ask his Maker's lenity.

July 14, 1867.

THOUGHTS OF HEAVEN.

At times the soul elastic springs
  From contact with its parent sod,
And borne upon devotion's wings
  Soars upward toward its God!

Forgotten then the cares of life,
  With nobler thoughts our bosoms swell,
Which raise us far above earth's strife,
  That drags us down to hell.

Would that this elevated mood
  Could oftener visit my poor heart,
And bid in holy solitude
  All grosser thoughts depart.

Then would I realize the dream
  That makes eternity appear
More blest than all that mortals deem
  Of earthly bliss most dear.

Sunday Night—Aug. 25, 1867.

SAD STORY IN VERSE OF "THE DOG AND THE RAKE."

A wild rake flew from Washington,
And brought his dog to Jefferson;
And when they reached the latter town
They called for chairs—and rake sat down.

And strange indeed it was to see
The dog, with collar marked " C. D.,"
Lay at the rake's feet his every bone,
Although the rake was not alone.

And then this dog got in a fight,
And rake rushed in with all his might;
And dealing blows both fair and foul,
He even made his own dog howl.

But soon the tide began to turn,
And rake, forlorn, began to yearn,
For lone he found himself—bereft,
But many a howler still was left.

That he might then the row appease,
He called aloud "Let us have peace!"
Alas! too late: the die was cast—
That rake's poor dog must breathe his last.

This made them only laugh right well,
A laugh that rake declared a yell;
But when his temper was restored,
It was his dog the cheers had bored.

This seedy rake, now left alone—
Because his dog was dead and gone—
He'd jumped to fire from frying-pan,
A sadder, if not wiser man!

When any boy has cake enough,
For that one boy to eat, he errs
If he behaves himself too rough,
And takes from other boys their *Schurz.*

DECORATION DAY AT ARLINGTON.

Let Arlington have peace,
    With flowers each tomb begem :
What scattering graves are these?
    Who is it weeps o'er them ?
A few lie buried here
    For whom pure tears are shed,
By mourners all sincere
    In grieving for their dead.

The lambs who went astray,
    Too near the butcher's shed,
A few who wore the grey
    Rest here close where they bled.
They perished near this spot,
    Brave martyrs to their cause ;
They fought for nothing not
    Vouchsafed them by the laws.

What! rebel-grief be shown
    So near the Royal Court?
Offensive to the throne,
    These vile ill-mannered sort!
Dare they come here with flowers?
    "Be soft, dear sir, we pray;
This custom, sir, is ours;
    You stole it from the grey."

God bids the flowers to blow,
    The dew and rain to fall,
The sun to shine, brooks flow,
    Alike for one and all.
But grief belongs alone
    To favored ones at Court:
"Brave soldiers—bayonets down
    That rebel mourner's throat!"

Strew salt upon the sod,
    Imperial, marine,
That even nature's God
    Deck no wrong grave with green.
Do robbers dread their slain,
    Lay bare their tombs to hate?
These forms may rise again,
    Retributive as fate.

Post guards at every grave,
  Despoil each garnished mound ;
Proud sentinel, armed slave,
  Guard well the stolen ground.
Suppress these rebels' grief,
  Let Arlington be glad ;
How dare their plundered chief
  O'er kindred bones be sad ?

Why should not rebels' grief
  On Arlington be shown ?
For who but Lee, their chief,
  These goodly acres own ?
Ancestral rebel sires
  Once wrested this same land
From royal occupiers,
  Imperial guardsman stand.

Through treason to the crown,
  To rightful flag and king,
Tradition has brought down
  The rights to which we cling.
The *loyal* were despised
  Two generations past ;
And *rebels* then comprized
  Nobility's true caste.

The lessons of to-day
  To future times belong;
See how the robbers pay
  For their successful wrong.
Rest, noble friends of Lee,
  Eternally repose;
Sleep where your ghosts can see
  Whole hecatombs of foes.

May, 1869.

YEARNINGS.

Earth and fame are a troubled dream ;
  Tell me for what is the heart still yearning :
Wealth and renown are not what they seem
  To the soul that in vain is for them burning.
All that the world can do is done,
  All it can give is mine;
But the eyes look up to the moon, and sun,
  And the stars that above us shine ;
And a thrill and a pang possess the heart,
And despair comes back with a flash-like start,
To teach how small a thing is life.
If this is the end and aim of strife—

This worthless, vain, vexatious story,
   In a world so tame, so drear—
   So brambled o'er with fear,
With naught secure, but that all must end—
Before we begin to comprehend
   The simplest end of being,
With every thing so flushed with doubt,
That sight itself is deceived about
   The thing it believes 'tis seeing.

June 29, 1869.

STRIVINGS.

Striving for something that cannot be,
   Longing for what can ne'er be won;
Trying to sound some fathomless sea,
   Climb to the moon, or soar to the sun;
Struggling to lift some moveless weight,
Battling against the laws of Fate;
Searching to find what none can show,
Seeking to know what none can know;
Tasking the brain, the hand, the heart,
Beyond all nature, beyond all art:
Such are the things that shorten the breath
Of fretful man, on his march to death.

And yet there are many things under the sun,
　　That men, who fail, might do right well ;
Things that would pay if right well done,
　　And worthy of those who failed and fell.
Working away with patient toil,
To wrest new fruits from the virgin soil;
Plodding along with quiet zeal,
To make some sad heart lighter feel ;
Planning home comforts for those we love,
Searching and working and looking above:
Such are the things that man can do,
To sweeten the lives of many and few.

IN AN ALBUM.

One word I'll leave before we part,
　　Upon this spotless page ;
One word that may thy faithful heart,
　　When absent, love, engage ;
A word whose music, like a spell,
　　Shall rival every sense,
And, near or far, shall ever tell
　　Of love's sweet recompense.

What shall that word so potent be,
    To thus all things combine,
Save this, that near or far from thee,
    Still darling, I am "Thine?"

THE BEST.

Of gems—the diamond I'd wear;
Of jewels—naught but cameos rare;
Of friends—I'd chose the one most true;
Of enemies—the knightliest too;
Of drinks—I'd take the royal wine;
Of robes—the purple hue divine;
Of air—the freshest; metals—gold;
Of followers—hearts devout and bold;
Of one to love—by land or sea,
Afar or near, I'd have but thee.

October 20, 1869.

EL LEON PENCIDO POREL HOMBRE.

Cierto artifice pinto.
Una lucha en que valiente

Un hombre tan solamente
A un horrible leon vencio :
Otro leon quel el cuadro vio
Sin preguntar por su autor
En tono despreciedor
Dijo ! bien se deja de ver
Que es pintar como querer.
Z no fue Leon el pintor.

TRANSLATION.

An artist in the days bygone
　　Painted a fight, in which a man,
In valiant struggle all alone,
　　Vanquished a lion fierce and tan.
Another lion saw the work,
　　And straight without a question said,
With a contemptuous tone and smirk :
　　" 'Tis easy here to see who spread
His wishes on the canvas centre ;
　　'Tis plain no lion was the painter."

Adversity, it is said, hath its uses. I doubt that; but while testing the preference I had for exile in Mexico over Yankee domination, I studied Spanish. Among other consoling things I found an old fable, a translation of which I respectfully dedicate to the newspaper reporters of the North.

November 9, 1869.

A Sunday Evening Reverie.

If God makes useful all that He has made,
When earth's ephemeral human race and earth
Have been and perished in the laspe of time,
What use can come of thoughtful souls in hell
If doubts require persuasion more than faith?
For 'tis a simpler task to yield belief,
And give no reason for the act of faith,
Than give good reason for suggested doubt;
Yet have some doubts a force we meet in vain—
Lives come into the world and pass away.
Whence come we? and what are we? whither bound?
The source, creation, is beyond our ken;
And what we are none know, yet all discourse—
And whither are we bound God knows, not we.
We argue for eternal life, because
It hurts our starveling vanity to die;
Yet no assurance e'er comes back to us
From the unknown hereafter, save the strains
Of weird imagination, and a faith
Rewarding our belief without a proof,
Of things so doubtful that all proofs we have
Are like the miracles ascribed to Jove.

He moulded with antiquity and the mist
Of heathen priest-craft, and the fabled tales
Of Roman or Egyptian auguries ;
And yet if these convince not, we are told,
Quite curtly too, sometimes with curse and threat,
Belief is right without a reason why ;
But reasoning without faith is heresy.
Is not intelligence the immortal part ?
Shall stupid goodness outlive daring wit,
And from the fixed emoluments of heaven
Soar forth to visit on angelic wings
The worlds that wicked doubters scoffed while here,
Revealing laws of God's organic skill,
And yet the knowing ones be chained in hell,
Able to teach what angels need to know,
Yet cast in useless darkness to endure
The torture they would ne'er inflict on brutes,
Because they were too wise to gloat on pain ?
'Tis a strange doctrine that to doubt is death,
Yet not more strange than that belief is life.
Both faith and reason are the gifts of God—
" Use one, ignore the other ; " madmen cry
" Believe or die ; " for if you can't believe,
Your death is well deserved, because you can't

Believe, because you do believe, and go
Straight up to heaven for service by and by,
Where such intelligence as *this* implies
Tends fit employment in celestial love.
And yet can they say this who say they think
That God's all governing control is such
That, infinite in being and in power,
He moulds all to His will, as plastic clay
Is moulded by the deft designer's touch.

November 21, 1869.

To the memory of that promising and untimely fate member of the
St. Louis bar,

MR. JABEZ L. NORTH.

Without a foe, without a fear,
Without a fault, a man sincere
  In all he thought and said ;
His was the loftiest, manly aim—
A useful life, devoid of blame,
  Unselfish, brave, well-bred.

Whate'er that future state may be,
When friends, revivified, shall see

.The friends held dear on earth;
Dear North! thy soul will join that band
Who love, in that celestial land,
Refinement, sense and worth.

To ——

Oh! lady, list the voice of one
Who would not lift a note of praise,
If outward loveliness alone
Required the tribute of his lays;
But when both heart and soul unite
To give to beauty's fleeting spell
A charm unutterably bright,
A something of immortal light,
No gifted tongue can tell—

How can I longer silent be?
Yet while I speak would counsel still,
That now and ever, fixed in thee,
Eternal truth may guide thy will!
So thoughts that in my bosom rest,
Soft heaving to a shrine so fair,

Shall be with holy fragrance blest,
  As dew-drops on the lily's breast
Imbibe a sweetness there!

Thus with a strength beyond thy years,
  In simple majesty of worth,
Thy soul shall tower above the fears
  And changing circumstance of earth.
Amid the cares that most annoy,
  Thou shalt in fadeless beauty shine;
For surely these cannot destroy,
  Nor stain the part without alloy,
The part which is divine!

January 16th, 1870.

HOME--SUNDAY,

To sing, and be happy in singing,
  The songs the cold-hearted disdain—
To spring, and be cheerful in springing,
  To soothe the distressed in their pain—
To give, and be joyful in giving,
  Relief to the wretched and weak—
Is life, while we live worth the living,
  Though all the world round us be bleak.

Jan. 20, 1870.

Arcana.

The golden glow of evening rays,
  Imprisoned by the burnished clouds,
Is milder than the mid-day blaze
  Of beams that flood the noon in crowds.

And thus the secret joys we build,
  Restricted boundaries though they own,
Are rosier than the hues that gild
  The glare of full-day's gaudy throne.

Feb. 24, 1870—In U. S. District Court Room.

To a Fifteenth Amendment Politician.

Go breathe the Afric scented air,
  Frequent polluted spots,
Caress the rabble every-where,
  Be friends with drunken sots.

Be called "great man" by lousy knaves,
  Until you think it true ;
Nor stop to think that Satan paves
  All hell with such as you.

Shrink from the gaze of decent men,
Compound with vice and shame;
Get office, steal, take gifts, and then
Call this success and fame.

April 14, 1870.

LINES.

[To an Imaginary Being.]

Far in the night I scan the bending sky,
To find the star of purest, brightest ray;
To center there the worship of mine eye,
Unheeding all the orbs that round it play:
So through the empyrean of my thoughts I turn,
And all save one fair planet thence I spurn.

Far in the night, when vigil lone I keep,
When eyes hold tears that lend the cheek a smile,
When foot-falls cease, and songs are hushed in sleep,
My soul takes wing, and flies to thee awhile;
To hover o'er thee, wheresoe'er thou art,
And seek its image mirrored in the heart.

Far in the night an influence I feel,
That links the mountain, river, lake, and plain

With lightning flash, without the thunder peal
    Transmitting.   " Passion is akin to pain."
And then a soundless voice, soft, sweet, and clear,
A message nameless whispers in mine ear.

Far in the night I loathe the splendid world,
    With daring thoughts despising all save thee,
Till hope, out-dazzled and unwinged, is hurled
    From heights Olympian to the Icarean sea;
From loftier realms than mortal pinions sweep,
Below despair's wide ocean, dark and deep.
July, 1870.

MASONIC COLLEGE, LEXINGTON, MO.

Battered and grim are thy classic walls,
Deserted and ruined thy murky halls,
    And the bats flit in and out.
Thy portals are gray with untimely decay,
And the windows are wasted and broken away,
    Where merry eyes once looked out.

Libraries, pictures, retorts, and the lore
In the laboratory's curious store,
    Were scattered by vandal hands.

A noble brotherhood's money and toil
Were destined to fall as the fruitless spoil
  Of the rabble of other lands.

Shade trees that sheltered our youthful play,
Remorselessly too have been all cut away,
  Replaced by the fort and ditch;
And in Liberty's name they give us the blame
Of defending our own from the forcible claim
  Of the Christians who burnt the witch.
21st Aug., 1870.

SAINT JOSEPH.

There's beauty in the River bend, when morning's
    early beam
Flings down its flood of light upon yon broad ma-
    jestic stream,
When cloudlets fleck the plain beyond with many
    a changing hue,
And Blacksnake hills receding melt in distance dim
    and blue.

There's beauty in the River bend, when noonday sun
    is high,

When earth seems struggling to reflect the glory of
   the sky,
Where steamers proudly move and breathe like
   things of life and power,
And every gaudy shrub puts forth its sweetlier
   pleading flower.

There's beauty in the River bend, when at the sunset glow
The gold and purple mount the sky and tinge the
   wave below,
When glowing wheels and clattering hoofs their
   cheerful music make,
And cheeks with honest crimson glow from driving
   to the lake.

There's beauty in the pictured dream of moonlit
   Prospect hill,
When, though afar, it seems to rise in vivid outline
   still,
And gives me back, through years and tears, the
   bright young form that stood
Beside me there—oh! vision rare! the brilliant and
   the good.

There's beauty in each starry hour, when night sup-
    plants the day,
And beauty still when drowned in light the planets
    sink away ;
By day, by night, by land or River bend, O ! city
    fair !
Thy children need but look to see there's beauty
    every-where.

St. Louis, Oct. 30, 1870.

THE RAINDROP.

I heard a little drop of rain
Fall on my darkened window pane,
And as it broke the silence there
Its whisper floated on the air.

That whisper, for it was no more,
A mystic revelation bore—
The lonely silence as it broke—
And these the words the raindrop spoke :

" Ten thousand years their labors lent
To form me in the firmament,
And every element a share
Contributed to fix me there.

" Thus bright and beautifully born,
With lines a rainbow to adorn,
My native realms appeared so high
I deemed my destiny the sky.

" But in the moment of my birth
I found myself impelled to earth,
And to my parent cycles cried,
In wild despair, my wounded pride.

" Is this the end of all your care,
Your tutelage in the upper air?
Were my creative hopes in vain?
Must I be merged in clouds and rain?"

The centuries this word returned:
" Think not thy beauties we have spurned,
For thee, all piteous as thou art,
There is a mission set apart.

" In this dark fall against thy will
Thou canst alone that mission fill;
And when apparently destroyed,
Thy uses first will be employed!

" Grand things depend upon the small,
Each part essential is to all ;
When seeming to oblivion hurled,
A raindrop helps revive a world !

" Thou shalt in other forms endure,
Ethereal, reproduced and pure ;
All parts of vast creation's plan
Are fixed by law—escape none can."

" Content with this, oblivion's host,
That perish, yet are never lost,
I joined with countless drops of rain,
And fell—yet who dare say in vain?"

Thus spoke the little drop of rain,
That whispered on my window pane,
And sparkling in the lamp light threw
A dying flash like diamond true.

" Celestial messenger," I cried,
" Since none in vain have lived and died,
Be death and dark oblivion mine,
The humblest misson is divine!"

Nov. 15, 1870.

Beauties of the Sky.

Oh! purple glow in the sunset sky!
Speak to the ear as thou dost to the eye,
And tell us the cause, and the reason why,
Thy fleeting and golden glories are given
To wrap the earth in the beauties of heaven.

Is silent beauty a useful thing?
Yea, it aids us to lift with angels the wing,
And to the sad soul sweet peace to bring;
Tho' it clothe not the needy, nor the hungry give
    food,
It wins the lone spirit to dwell with the good.
1871.

Blair's First Speech in the Senate.

One giant yet is left,
  Colossal in the land,
To prove the antique models cleft
  In marble pure and grand,
Were proto-types of this our day,
Foretold in ages passed away.
    Bravo for Blair!

"Republic" is a name
  Aspiring chieftains hate;
Monopolists of wealth and fame
  Must overthrow the state.
Oh! for one hero in such hour,
To check the growth of one-man power.
      Bravo for Blair!

One voice at last is heard,
  Designing schemes to mar;
One freeman, faithful to his word,
  In peace as well as war—
As fearless in the senate-hall
As facing shell and minnie-ball.
      Bravo for Blair!

Needs man a master yet?
  Deserve we this disgrace?
Can foeman trust the bayonet
  At freedom's voting place?
If these be needful, danger still
Reposes in the people's will!
      Bravo for Blair!

Down with the tyrant's plea,
  Down with the bristling arms!

While these remain, not all are free
   From despotism's harms.
Armed innovations we condemn,
Let those trust us—not we trust them.
      Bravo for Blair !

Feb. 15, 1871.

THE MOUNTAIN SPRING.

A mountain spring far inland, to a hermit passing by,
In plaintive whisper murmured, " I believe I will go
   dry ;
I see no use in struggling to maintain a brooklet here,
For birds and beasts but rarely come, and no one
   else comes near.

" Besides, I am obscure and small, while all the
   world takes pride
In grand expensive reservoirs, and rivers full and
   wide ;
To commerce I am worthless, for no bark could float
   on me,
Nor do I think one drop of mine can ever reach the
   sea."

Then said the hermit to the spring, "Your story I
    have heard,
But think you 'tis a little thing to soothe a little bird?
If from the world's creation you had flowed un-
    touched and clear,
One sip to cool some tongue athirst were worth
    your being here.

"Should every little thing refuse to do what good it
    can,
How soon the infinite result would spoil the general
    plan;
Then do your duty, little spring, send forth your
    waters bright,
Each one of multitudes like you makes up the
    ocean's might."

Feb. 17, 1871.

THE TEETOTALER'S IDEAL BIBATION.

O! give me some delicate wine,
    Less gross than the rosy Moselle,
Whose flavor like nectar divine
    Will everything mortal dispel;
Not something that flushes,

But something that hushes,
　　The red tide of life in the breast—
To gently o'ercome me,
And gently benumb me,
　　Until I feel willing to rest.

There is none so exquisite made—
　　Then no tempting poison for me !
Give spurs to the scrub and the jade,
　　But let the free courser run free.
If there is none of it,
This wine that I covet,
　　No counterfeit fluid I'll taste ;
If manhood claims glory,
What shame in the story
　　Of primitive manhood debased.

Then give me some delicate wine,
　　To soothe and to quiet rude care ;
For something exalting I pine,
　　When pressed by my burden of care ;
And yet something harmless and fine,
　　Unfollowed by ache or despair ;
So cheap that to drink it
Will not make me think it

A selfish indulgence of mine.
Not taxed until scanty,
But flowing and plenty—
Cold water is God's chosen wine.

March 6, 1871.

A PURE NAME.

Among the maids immortal born,
  To shine in glory's blazing sky,
Till glory fades in Heaven's morn,
  Thy name shall be the last to die.

O keep it ever fair and pure!
  Unstained and spotless, as sublime,
That while its music shall endure
  'Twill sweeten with the lapse of time;

Transmitting to an age remote,
  In thy example, marked and known,
One brilliant type that shall denote
  The heart wherein thou hast thy throne—

That will in days far hence inspire
  The tempted maid from vice and shame,

And woo to virtue and to bliss—
　To that age be, as thou to this.

When Time assails thy gentle brow,
　And Pain's unsparing hand takes hold,
Thou will be young in fame as now
　Thy wisdom seemeth old.

May 11, 1871.

The Adieu of a Graduate.

Like barks that from one port have sailed
　To trace the ocean's devious breast,
Where storms have over all prevailed,
　And few have found success and rest :
So we life's ocean now must try,
　Not knowing what may lie before,
And only able to descry
　The outlines of receding shore.

Some will be beckoned to the West,
　And some the Orient will woo ;
But all will love the home port best,
　And bless its *terra firma* true.

Life's ocean glows with luring lights,
That signal us to different ways,
But like fixed stars in azure heights
Shine precepts learned in youthful days.

Celestial faith—our Polar Star—
May reach with its divergent ray
Our several hearts, tho' sundered far,
And safely guide our wandering way.
And so will HE, who doth all well,
Our destinies remote unite,
As o'er the ocean's wide, wide swell,
One sky tucks in the world at night.

As doth HIS all-uniting love
Reveal to our uplifted gaze
One shining heaven that bends above,
And downward lets its glories blaze :
So souls that tremble toward HIS throne,
HE unifies and makes HIS own,
That present, absent, near or far,
They gaze alike on one fixed star ;
And influenced by its rays serene,
Feel near—though oceans roll between.

June 12, 1871.

THE IDEAL.

Within my heart an image dwells,
　Too beauteous for the limner's skill;
Whose power each rising passion quells,
　And bids my stormy soul—be still!

Not all the craft of Raphael's brush
　To canvas could that face transfer;
Nor is there need of light to flush
　Its features o'er with radiance clear.

At midnight hour its glow is bright
　As when its tints defy the sun;
No darkness can obscure the light
　It sheds for me—when day is done.

For me it shines—for me alone—
　Its sacred beauty is for me;
Does it resemble any one?
　Yes, darling—it but copies thee.

June 12, 1872.

IMAGINARY.

Another year! Another year!
And thou art there, and I am here;

The days, the nights, the weeks are gone,
The months to age-like ends have drawn;
The vernal buds, the summer leaves,
The birds that sang o'er autumn sheaves,
Have come and gone, and hated snow
Recalls the flakes of bitter woe
That fell and froze—a year ago.

Another year! Another year!
And thou art there, and I am here;
Again the flakes seem downward driven,
Like curses thick from vengeful Heaven;
Yet still I cling, with desperate hand,
To hope's poor crumbling rope of sand,
As drowning sailors, chilled and numb—
Not speechless, only faint and dumb—
Not lifeless, drift—and dream of home.

Another year! Another year!
And thou art there, and I am here;
And ah! when we were forced to part,
Had some weird vision told my heart
That I could live to see this day,
With thee, my life, my soul, away—

Away and silent—I would fain
Have summon all up in one short pain,
Before the snow had fallen again.

Another year !   Another year !
And thou art there, and I am here;
'Tis said we must be purified,
As metal in the fire is tried ;
That suffering in this world of strife
Is discipline for higher life :
I know not, care not, seek not bliss
Attained at such a cost as this;
I crave no Heaven beyond thy kiss !

Another year !   Another year !
And thou art there, and I am here;
E'en yet word music lingers still,
Like echo on some distant hill ;
And thoughts that were all crude before,
Entombed like shapeless hoards of ore
In nature's rich, yet dingy mine,
Have through this furnace, love, of thine,
Been moulded into shapes divine.

Jan. 1st, 1873.

In Memory of Chas. R. Davis.

The uplifted hand of the smiter
   Hangs heavy and sore over all ;
It strikes down the reader and writer,
   It spares not the great nor the small ;
But the blow seems more dire and unsparing,
   And grief seems the hardest to bear,
When the gifted, the good and the daring,
   Are torn from the world they make fair.

There's a gap in the phalanx of labor,
   A rift in a chain hard to mend ;
The scholar, the thinker, the neighbor,
   No less to be mourned than the friend ;
The good and the manly will miss him,
   As one of their boldest and best ;
But alas ! for the lips that will kiss him,
   And lay him away to his rest.

St. Louis, July 21, 1873.

Poor Davis ! the last time I saw him he was well and hearty at the frolic at the Globe's First Anniversary. That was Friday, 18th. Monday I wrote the above lines, upon hearing of his death.— A. W. S.

A Coquette.

"I have no heart, and this," she said,
  "I told you long ago;
I've torn it piecemeal, shred by shred—
Its pulse is there, its feeling dead.
Extinct volcanoes mostly know
The regions of supernal snow.
        Call words but breath;
        There is no faith."
  Stop! say not so.   Ah! say not so!

."I've changed my mind, and you," she said,
  "Can do the same, you know.
My kisses will not linger long,
And you can find relief in song.
The poet's soul was made to know
The heights of joy, the depths of woe:
        The callous breast
        Allures him best."
  Stop! say not so.   Ah! say not so!

"If you must love, you can," she said,
"Love some one else, you know.
The world is full of beauteous flowers;
Go seek them in more welcome bowers;

Woo some one else, and let me go
My ways—I have enough to do ;
    Time lost, I dare
    No longer spare."
Stop ! say not so.   Ah ! say not so!
Dec. 3, 1873.

WISH YOU MY NAME.
Answer to a French Song.

Wish you my name?   It is for thee !
Wish you my goods?   They too are thine !
    With all my heart I give them thee,
If your bright eyes on me will shine,
    If you'll repose awhile with me,
    That you may know how I love thee.
Ah ! that you knew how I love you !

    Wish you my heart?   It is for you ;
'Tis just as well that you should know
    That I have nothing—nothing, dear—
Nothing that can to me pertain
    That is not thine by title clear.
Ah ! take my heart ! It is for you :
    If only *how I love*, you knew ;
    If *how* I love, you only knew !
1873.

ASPIRATION.

To mould some thought, to say some word,
Above, beyond, the common herd,
Whose fame would live in after-time—
Some act, some utterance sublime,
Some teaching to lift up mankind,
Some precept lofty and refined,
Some plea for love to everything
That nature dooms to suffering,
Or bold rebuke of human wrong,
No matter where the fault belong—
To do, to say, to think, to write,
Some novel thing each day and night,
Yet leave behind some sample best
To live, as token of the rest,
Expression of the homage due
From faithful heart to heart as true :
Be this my life's ambition high,
To cheer me when I come to die.

July 30, 1873.

LINES,
To a Pretty Teacher of the French Language.

While tints that tinge the autumn woods
Lend beauty to the hill and plain,

Teach me thy tenses and thy moods,
　　Let me thy charming accent gain :
Lead me not into poet's page,
But read from some Platonic sage.

" *Tres bien ;* " the wise Confucius said,
　　"Be calm ; observe the ' *au mileau.*' "
Ah ! had he seen thy classic head,
　　Or felt thine eyes of dazzling blue,
The wisest ancient would have known
He could not call his heart his own.

" Act when alone as if ten eyes
　　Were on you with ten pointing hands."
'Tis easy to philosophize
　　On something no one understands :
Could he have seen thy hands of snow,
He would have let all others go.

" Keep your affections well controlled,
　　O ! Prince, if you would govern well."
The sage's words are wise and bold ;
　　His princess never knew the spell
That swells the bosom of a bard,
Beneath thy magic " *prenez garde.*"

" Say nothing you would wish to change,"
    The prudent old preceptor taught;
But had he come within thy range,
    Thy glance would many a vow have caught;
And then, as from thy mirth he fled,
He would have wished his words unsaid.

So on, we might the page pursue,
    But why redouble proofs so plain?
Confucius never dreamed of you,
    Nor studied French on railway train:
His old philosophy was fine,
But modern learning is divine.

Oct. 30, 1873.

TOO SWIFT.

Ah! stay your flight, evasive hours,
    And linger once with folded wings;
Forbear with swiftly hastening powers
    To speed the bliss that loving brings.
Be fleet with those who suffer ill,
    Be spoilers where they wish thee gone;
But bid the sun of life stand still,
    While love's soft spell is round me drawn.

Let each dear glance consume a day,
   Let each fond word an hour destroy ;
While to replace each tress astray
   A month caressingly employ.
Life is but laughter, love and tears,
   With laughter then and tears be swift;
But linger out the happy years—
   This glimpse of Heaven through clouds arift.

March 3, 1874.

BETRAYAL.

What fiend Plutonic nerves the arm
That does the unsuspecting harm,
And injuries that have no end
Inflicts upon a bosom friend !

To cast a shade on shining name,
To doom to ruin rising fame,
To plant the wound, so hard to heal,
On side exposed to treacherous steel!

All these are base, but baser still
Is he whose smile betides no ill,
Invites the trust of winsome maid,
And ruins, ere he makes afraid.

Ah ! woe to him who can betray
The faith that flings mistrust away ;
For shuddering demons cannot tell
A crime more hideous in hell.

May, 1874.

TO AN IMAGINARY CORRESPONDENT.

What answer?   Not a word or line !
  Though oft I've called to thee ;
There does not come a single sign
  From yonder soundless sea.
No echo even to the words
  From parted lips that fly,
Yet perish like the laden birds
  That on the desert die.

In anguish all complaint is hushed,
  Except the voice of song,
And that I've stifled back and crushed
  With struggles fierce and strong,
Until, like some resistless tide,
  That sweeps down every stay,
Wild numbers burst the bounds of pride,
  And dash restraint away.

When thus the mastery is o'erthrown
    In duty's desolate domain,
The only solace to me known
    Has been to yield the strife so vain,
And, looking up in mortal woe,
    Appeal to God for strength to bear
The burden that no heart can know,
    And none, save thine and mine, can share.

May 2, 1874.

"MY SHRINE."

Upon my mantel, in a row,
Four simple pictures glow,
With shining frames about them placed
Of neat and modest taste;
Four images of daughters mine,
Four little darlings, rare and fine,
Whose faces beam with light divine—
And here I've made my shrine.

The place is more like sacred ground
Than any I have found;
No dome of fresco reared by art
Can so impress my heart:

'Tis here I feel remorse begin,
With contrite grief for every sin;
And faults that, close to crime akin,
Make heaven so hard to win.

And here my soul, remote from crowds,
Is shadowed by no clouds;
Aloof at last from tangling care,
I lift to God my prayer;
And He that doth in secret see
In secret seems to answer me,
For sake of these, that I may be
From secret sin kept free.

Alone, I seek at this pure shrine
The face of God divine.
In public no one is sincere,
For all are tinged with fear;
But here my heart is all laid bare
To Him who doth for sparrow care;
To him I lift a parent's prayer—
" Wilt Thou these children spare!

" May they be happy in their loves,
And innocent as doves;

May they, as daughters, sweethearts, wives,
Be honest in their lives;
And while none others they deceive,
Lead them no falsehoods to believe,
That might, too late, their spirits grieve—
Poor drifting bairns of Eve!

"Of wicked vice, debased and low,
Let them not even know;
Like their own mother, let them be
From affectation free;
And ere their dying lips are dumb
Grant them faith's victory o'er the tomb,
And let them to Thy kingdom come
In yonder heavenly home."

This is my prayer, I say and feel,
As at my shrine I kneel;
And lo! though absent far and wide,
I think them at my side;
And hosts celestial come and go,
On radiant wings as white as snow,
Till heaven above and heaven below
Have made my shrine aglow.

But no intruding eye could see
The light that shines on me ;
For little pictures on the wall
To others would be all ;
And yet to me the thought is given
Of such the kingdom is of heaven ;
And from this shrine despair is driven
By hope to be forgiven.

Aug. 28, 1874.

INDIAN SUMMER.

The russet, brown October leaves
  The frost and sun are tinging o'er,
And safe amid the garnered sheaves
  The field mouse hides her winter's store.
The spider mounts her gauzy stair,
  Her flight on home-made wings she lifts,
And lazy on the languid air
  A fleecy cloud at random drifts.

Through azure depths the sunbeams pour
  On woodlands crowned with gorgeous dyes,
And town and village raise once more
  Their smoky columns toward the skies.

What is it in this autumn scene
    That from the past seems asking me
If it was summer—that has been?
    If it is winter—that must be?

I know not! yet a voice is gone,
    Whose tones gave music to the spring;
And dreary months must hope, hope on,
    Ere back again that voice 'twill bring.
I know not! yet remember well
    The summer warmth, and glow, and light
That once on such a day befell
    A heart now plunged in gloom and night.
I know not! yet the past has shown
    That leaves may wither, snows may fall,
Yet love be faithful to its own,
    And hearts be changeless after all.

October 13, 1874.

ARTHUR BARRETT'S FUNERAL.

A mournful dirge swells from the street,
    From lofty spires the bells are tolling—
And, followed by slow marching feet,
    The voiceless, stately hearse is rolling.

Chief magistrate of mighty city,
    Fresh from the victory and the strife ;
Love, hate, revenge, all melt to pity,
    For such an end to such a life.

But deeper than all outward grieving
    Feel those hot eyes whence tears have fled ;
Who loved less Mayor than man when living,
    And mourn the man, not Mayor, when dead !

April 27, 1875.

A Curiosity of Rhyme.

Where Ignorance is Bliss, 'tis Voullaire to be Wise :
So Sharpe a Jeck-O ! who will Kreiter-cise ?
Cunningham argument studied Knight and Day ;
No Wag-nor Duke can always hold at Bay !
For High or Lowe, in Comfort or in Payne,
The ousters *Spes* will be to oust again.
The Wolff of Justice, Poepping from her Wood,
Dis- Arm-strong Kehrs, and Knox them into Goode ;
She comes, and on her comes a pilgrim Grey,
To Deck-er turf—perhaps to rob Barclay !
To Fletch-er bacon, or her Castle-burry,

With gifts to flatter, rich and grey and very.
The time for Vast-ine-terments is at hand;
The Jew-ett cetera join our band.
Beyond what lawyers get for fees (except Black-
    Jerry)   ·
Will bring down wrathful verdicts in a hurry.
Be Mum-for to decay disposed no saint,
Nor sinner either, can Espy life's taint
In time to Shield the insatiate Archer's Blow,
When at his Marks the Bowman bends his bow.
Long Daily to be free,
Those who bow and smile and bend the knee
To Rankin Posts with Bishop and Pope,
Rum-bower Peeples with every hope.
The Ewing Birds Light-high-sir, when they soar;
O'Kneel! and Polk your Dryden fun no Moore.
To Taussig, Noble, Smiths, with Brown Redd hands,
Pay Williams' Sterling, but pay *bills* to Shands;
And Broadhead bands by Garish aid make Chase.
With Gantt-let Glove-or magisterial Mace.
Although no Mauro rainbow of the past be seen,
From Snowy White to Hughes of Brown and Green,
Keep Cullen's Kitchen Gardiners in close sight—
You are no Peacock, but a Clay-born wight.

Carroll and Whittle cedar as he goes,

Dismiss his muse and prosecute his prose;

Like Law-rents, when Higged-on, imp-Loring cries,

Will whisk down judgment from the wrathful skies;

And Treat with Dyer contempt all rules of Wright,

To right the wrong of what you write to-night.

Will Hitch-cock-ades of Clover, Brown and Gray,

Till Fields of Corne-will Woods of Moss display.

Audacious Bard, I bid you now be-Ware,

Such liberties with names no Page will bear;

You must not Lett-on at such a Boyle-ing rate,

A new Reber Bell-ion you'll inaugurate.

It was the intention of Col. Slayback to place the names of all
the Lawyers at the Bar in this piece, but it was never finished,
and some lines had to be left out on that account.

THE DEAD JUDGE.

He was a learned man—with ease could quote

All kinds of fine things he had learned by rote;

And as to law, he knew it, and could feel

As sure as we do, when we take appeal:

And searching books would somehow always find,

Without convincing his own mind,

That if the court should decide
Against him, he their ruling must abide.
He had his faults, but these we will not name,
'Tis only of his virtues we declaim;
And yet, upon reflection, we admit
He somewhat spoilt all these with traits not fit
To expatiate upon just now, but still
'Tis only fair to those in grief to tell
The usual, customed and respected lie,
That we condole with them, yet all must die;
And since his turn mysteriously came first,
Surviving hearts should struggle not to burst
With hopeless sorrow, and will feel less bad,
Apologizing for the faults he had.
With this view only we will name a few
For which he was distinguished, and review—
" *De mortuis nil* "—and so forth, lest some head
Might take the notion we disliked the dead;
But for the instruction of surviving youth,
And for the warning, we must say in truth,
That this man viciously sat up at night,
Hours that belonged to sleep, and then would write
Some things 'twere best they were unwritten quite.
He was, unfortunately, much inclined

On painful subjects too to speak his mind ;
And that was not the best of minds always,
We solemnly admit, tho' prone now but to praise.

Still he is gone, and what he's done is done :
I move committees, to consist of one,
Each court of record shall the judges bore
By a recital of what we now deplore ;
And also one to find if there be those
Dependent on him needy in their woes—
That some of us may, 'spite this heterodoxy,
Attend his funeral, and give cash by proxy.

This speech elicited subdued applause,
And buzzing sanction filled the ensuing pause,
When up there rose a face with busier turn,
And moved that, *sine die*, "we adjourn."
1875.

THE UNDERTAKER.

By onerous profits wreaked from the distressed,
Who count not cost while grief distracts the breast,
The crafty oppressor drives his gilded hearse,
And adds to death's bereavement one more curse :

The costly pomp of fashionable grief,
That grasps from sorrow what would shame a thief;
The impoverished widow and her orphans sigh
For him who died, and what he cost to die.

THE DEPARTED.

The busy wheels roll o'er the humming street,
The sidewalks echo to the tread of feet,
New faces come and go and pass away,
And those we miss are missed but for a day;
And those who stir and meet and greet awhile,
And feverish hours with cares intense beguile,
Are hastening, hurrying dust unto its dust,
To prove belief less strange than cold mistrust.

1875.

SOME MISTAKEN PROPHECIES.

You said that time would change my heart,
    That tender words were frail as air;
You said that should our pathways part,
    We soon would learn to love elsewhere;

But long, long years have passed since then,
   And we have wandered devious ways,
Yet none among adoring men
   Has loved as I have loved always.

You said by searching I would find
   Some hand more free, some eye more blue,
Some soul as beautiful and kind,
   Some heart as tender and as true ;
Yet every fair one I have met
   Has brought to memory anew
The charms I never can forget,
   The loveliness supreme in you.

You said if time should prove you wrong,
   Some future day you might incline
To listen to my sad love song,
   And may be then you could be mine ;
And joys divine it brings to me
   To know that, when my hand you press,
It is not in your heart to be
   Unmindful of my faithfulness.

Sept. 11, 1875.

GRIEF.

Within each human heart there dwells
  Some grief too bitter to be told,
Some sorrow that no token tells,
  Nor eye intrusive can behold.

And yet the pangs we thus conceal
  Would never be so keenly felt,
Did not the conscious bosom feel
  Its silence half way due to guilt.

A phantom enters, saying " you did right"—
  Another passes, saying " no, 'twas wrong "—
And thus throughout the sleepless, wretched night,
  Disputing thoughts their arguments prolong ;
Thus hearts must throb until return of light,
  " Who learn through suffering what they teach in
    song."

Dec. 6, 1875.

IMAGINARY.

When round me all the world is gay
  With sounds of gladness, scenes of mirth,

The thought that thou art far away
   Makes love too sad a thing for earth.

At such a time I feel how lone,
   How far from sympathy I dwell,
And pine for joys no longer known,
   With sorrow that no tongue can tell.

'Tis then that most I miss the one
   Who wears Elysium in her face;
My heart's adored! my *queen!* my own!
   Who gives to life its only grace.

'Tis then, my best beloved, I ache
   To know if I'm best loved by thee,
And wonder if a heart can break
   While vainly struggling to be free.

'Tis then I sink from self away,
   And plunge in waves of wordly care,
Regardless how the storms may play
   Above the billows of despair.

Dec. 30, 1875.

A COMMON LOT.

Oft in the heart a secret lies
   Unuttered and unshown,

That neither tongue, nor lips, nor eyes,
  Nor hand, nor face makes known.

Oft in the breast a passion dwells,
  That makes or mars a life ;
Yet not one outward signal tells
  The inward fire and strife.

Oft in the soul, devotion's eye
  Its constant vigil keeps,
With tenderness that cannot die,
  And zeal that never sleeps.

Oft in the brain a purpose lives,
  Heroic and divine,
That courage all enduring gives
  To die—and make no sign.

Dec. 1, 1876.

UNREST.

Sick at heart and sore of brain,
Weary of a heart so vain—
Jaded down with worldly strife,
With its madd'ning thrusts at life,

With its war upon the good,
With its base ingratitude,
With its ever fickle praise,
With its carping blame always—
With its doubtful, slow rewards,
With its doom-like, lost regards—
With its over-rated gold,
Hard to get, and hard to hold—
With its gems, so bright, so vain,
Easier lost than to attain—
With its horrors, dark and dread,
With its struggles fierce for bread—
With its scandal to provoke
Character-assailing joke—
Smile derisive of disdain,
Frown so gloomful like with pain—
Sudden pangs and fleeting joys,
Life filled up with sham deploys:
Where shall unrest find an end?
Who can joy and blessing send?
Shall the soul e'er seek in vain
Antidote for earth's dark bane?

ANTICIPATION.

Will the thoughts of the by-gone years come back?
  Will the boyhood dreams return?
When honor and truth laid down the track
  For zeal and youth to devoutly yearn
  To run upon, and the prize to earn,
  In the world's great race for fame?

Will the love that was honest and faithful last?
  Will it live when others die?
Will the cold world enter with chilling blast
  The precincts warm of my loving heart,
  When the world I knew was a world apart
  From this cheerless place of sin?

Will the faith that made youth so fair grow dim?
  Will it all dissolve in doubt?
Will the great world's music make the hymn
  My mother sang less grand and fine
  When my ear grows used to the strains divine
  Of the organ's thundering tone?

Will the bliss of my boyhood joy still live
  When the wise old age has come?
Will the conflagration flame and live

When the fires of strife have raged and rolled ?
Will ambition's torch be out and cold
That enkindled all this blaze ?
Jan. 12, 1877.

LAKE MINNETONKA.

All quiet on the azure lake the summer sunshine lay,
And fair upon its bluish waves the sail-boats gem-
    med the bay;
The flowers beside the roadway gave the air a sweet
    perfume,
And far more fair than they was she who watched
    with me their bloom.

The summer flowers have faded now along the lake-
    side shore,
And she who breathed their incense then is at my
    side no more ;
The sails that gemmed the bay are gone far o'er the
    shining waves,
And hopes that then were rich with joy are dead in
    hopeless graves.

The summer breeze for me no more its incense soft
    can shed,
The heart that made it sweet is broke and faith is
    lost and dead ;
'Tis winter all year round, so drear, so desolate and
    chill—
I bow to Fate, and live, because pain has no power
    to kill!

Dec. 15, 1877.

———

To ——.

When sorrow comes to grieve thy heart,
    Remember joy cannot be far ;
As clouds and skies are not apart,
    And past them all there beams a star.
When shadows wrap the earth in gloom,
    The other half is bright and fair ;
And human grief has flowers which bloom
    Within the forests of despair.

April 16, 1878.

———

UNSATISFIED.

Familiar to the trump of Fame,
    The world's applause around him rang ;

And lavish Fortune lent a name
    That nations praised and poets sang.

His blazing jewels could not bring
    A moment's glance at peaceful rest ;
His brain was but a burning thing,
    A smouldering fire consumes his breast.

But Pomp, with all its empty toys,
    And Wealth, with all its gilded pride,
Were inward griefs, though outward joys—
    His heart remained unsatisfied.
1878.

On Reading Faces.

"Papa, when lawyers have to choose,
    From men they do not know,
Good jurors, who will not abuse
    Their oaths, how do they do?"

So asked a little eight-year old,*
    As she half closed a book,
And, flinging back her locks of gold,
    A poise expectant took.

*Minnette.

" What curious questions children ask ! "
    Said Papa with a smile ;
" To answer rightly is a task
    That sometimes takes a while."

'Tis hard to read men by their looks,
    The bad look like the good ;
And yet they may be read like books,
    When they are understood—

For still there is a sort of glance
    That lurks in every face,
Which does not leave us all to chance,
    If we know how to guess.

And though there is no settled rule
    To read men by their eyes,
Each day we live is but a school
    To see through all disguise.

And if a man be bad at heart
    And willing to do wrong,
He rarely has sufficient art
    To fool us very long.

So by and by the face is old,
    Each wrinkle, line and glance,

Its faithful story well has told—
  'Tis rarely there by chance :

For many a little meanness,
  And many a sneaking theft,
Upon his smirking features
  Its tell-tale line has left.

Nay, more ! the silent work of time
  Goes on from day to day ;
Each good thought leaves a trace sublime—
  Each bad, the other way.

And though he try to look serene,
  His efforts will betray
Some latent symptom that is mean,
  Which gives him clear away.

Beneath the silent work of time
  The features wear away ;
They grovel, or become sublime,
  By night, from day to day.

Goodness will cause the face to be
  The type of deeds well meant,
While evil hearts are never free
  From trace of bad intent.

Therefore, my darling little child,
    Be watchful how you act;
For even if the thoughts are wild,
    The face will show the fact.

Thus will the soul-life give its form
    And meaning to the eyes;
As trees will fall which way the storm
    Has swept across the skies.

But 'tis hard to tell men by their looks
    With any certitude;
Of every twelve men in the box,
    There will be bad and good.

Feb. 9, 1879.

TO MY DAUGHTER MINNETTE.

Ever be blameless—thus you'll be free—
    None but the wicked are slaves;
None but the innocent ever can be
    Worthy to fill honored graves.

Only the blameless are fit to be free,
    Only the faithful are wise;
We learn to command when we learn to obey;
    Through duty alone can we rise.

March 2, 1879.

To Brother A. V. C. S.*

It may be a little late in the day
    To wish you a Happy New Year ;
But still I must waive at you, far away,
    With a heartfelt friendly cheer.

'Tis vain to look back, or too far ahead,
    Our vision has narrow range ;
So let us be friends till life is fled,
    Without any cooling change.

There must come a time—
God grant not soon—
    When one will miss the other ;
But until it comes, let us prize the boon
    Of knowing and loving a BROTHER.

Jan. 7, 1880.

To Darling Grace.

Let me never fail to find
    Sweet sympathy in thee,
And I will strive to be resigned
    To all fate has for me.

1880.

---

*Rev. A. V. C. Schenck, Philadelphia.

BE MERRY.

Then let us laugh, and
Then let us eat, drink, laugh;
Then let us fret no more for fame.
Why should mortals fret for fame,
Or turn from homely fun with shame,
When laughter, merriment and song
To living joy alone belong?
The melancholy too must die;
'Tis better then to laugh than cry.

1880.

FRET NOT.

Fret not—the world will someway wag along,
  Until the blunders will be made all right;
The pigmy truth will kill the giant wrong,
  As David slew Goliah in the fight.

Grieve not—those only mourn who fail to see
  The sweet, but needful, uses of ill fate;
And way beyond the breakers of the sea
  Sail ships of hope, all full of precious freight.

1880.

Home Pleasures.

[To Mabel.]

We never know what home is worth,
  Until we go away;
We never know the need of light,
  Until the close of day.

1880.

"De Mortuis Nil," Etc.

"The *Times* is dead," the carrier said,
  With a doleful voice and mien;
"But no one thought it ever ought
  Such cruel fate to have seen."

"What do you intend, my doleful friend?"
  The old subscriber said:
"Do you mean to state there is any fate
  More cruel than being dead?"

Why yes, indeed; after death had freed
  The *Times* from all its woe,
Its awful remains, including brains,
  Were exposed to buzzard and crow.

The buzzard flapped its wings, and snapped
　　The flesh from off the bones ;
And then the crow for the bones did go,
　　And cawed in dismal tones.

" And so I say," said the carrier grey,
　　" It looks quite sad, my friend,
To see the pair of vultures tear
　　The corpse up at the end."

Jan. 1, 1881.

THERE'S NOTHING IN THIS VALE OF TEARS.

There's nothing in this vale of tears, as dearly as
　　we love it,
But takes its beauty from the spheres that roll on
　　high above it ;
If stars, which shine so fair and bright, should from
　　the skies be driven,
The fairest beauties of the night would be no
　　longer given.

Next take the moon, celestial queen,
　　The Heavenly orbs transcending ;
And lover's walks and moonlight scene
　　Must straightway find an ending.

Obscure the sun, celestial King,
  Of light and color the dispenser;
And earth contains no living thing—
  Her ashes lie in shattered censer.

Oh! let the broken words, impelled
  By quivering lips and aching heart,
Recall the rising passion quelled,
  Restore the pangs regrets impart.

TO A LEARNED ATHEIST.

Bright indeed are the flashes of genius,
Yet bright like the flash of a gun,
That shines far away in the darkness,
But cannot be seen in the sun.
The knowledge men have has been added
By little and little to stores
Of wisdom, as gems of the ocean
Have washed into heaps on the shores.
There is something sublime in the teachings
That men gather up from the past,
But the lessons they glean from the present
Are lessons more useful at last.

What happened to Cyrus and Cæsar
Of old on the land or the sea,
Have little to change of the ventures
That happen to you or to me.
The sun and the moon and the planets
Roll on in the depths of the sky,
And there they will roll in the ages
Long after all mortals shall die.
The most we can know is so feeble,
So full of misgiving and doubt,
That the best we can do is to trust Him
Who brought all we know about.

November 2, 1881.

The above was written on reading the discussion between Col.
Robert Ingersoll and Judge Jere. Black.

TO SLEEP.

O, sleep! so sweet to mortal eyes,
Enfold me with thy gentle wings,
And let me feel the rest that brings
Earth's throbbing heart to paradise.

Now fold me in thine angel wings,
O, sleep! so sweet to mortal eyes,
And let me feel the rest that brings
The weary soul its paradise.

November 19, 1881.

FOUND IN "DEMOSTHENES,"

AFTER HIS DEATH.

Stir not the latent pangs
  Sleeping within my heart;
Memory hath venomed fangs,
  Bid them not start.
Discord alone it brings,
Striking discordant strings—
Passions deal sufferings.
  Then bid me not recall
Scenes that are fading fast—
  Let them be banished all.

KNOWLEDGE.

Bring in thy sheaves, the day is done,
  Fate's mandate is condign;
  What has been gleaned is thine,
But what is left, by others must be won.

Crave not the things that might have been,
  Fret not at chances lost;
  Count up the gain, the cost,
And sigh no more to work or strive or win.

An end, an end for all must come,
  To win, to lose, are past;
  The end must come at last—
Who fights with fate fights only to succumb.

Life is but one long, anxious day,
  Whose hours are sure to close;
  With work still left for those
Who choose the worthy or the useful way.

Then give to me all things to know,
  Of good and evil too;
  To our first parents true,
This fruit I'll taste, from Eden though I go.

1881.

MAN A CONTRADICTION.

When silence broods upon the night,
    Our thoughts, like soldiers roused, are loud;
And though alone we feel the light
    Of noon, and hear its busy crowd.

There is no way to count on Fate,
    Or drive the shadows from our side;
We love the things we ought to hate,
    Exult when shame should banish pride.

The infant's breath is soonest out,
    And Life to Death stands ever near;
For Faith itself is full of doubt,
    And Hope has everything to fear.

We crave for poison, shun our food,
    And strive for that which brings but ill;
We spurn the things that do us good,
    And seek for cure in things that kill.

The things we toil for clog when won,
    We count but poor the joys we gain;
We grope beneath the noonday sun,
    And laugh at danger and at pain.

Jan. 12, 1882.

TO MY DAUGHTER KATIE.

May peace and joy thy steps attend,
   Dear Katie, gentle, darling child ;
   And God our Heavenly Father, mild,
Be ever near thee, as a friend.

May all thy thoughts be free from sin,
   And all thy actions free from wrong ;
   And may thy life be sweet and long,
And at its close may Heaven begin.

Jan. 16, 1882.

SPEAK GENTLY.

What can the head do rightly
   When the heart is afire with pain ?
And how can the mind think brightly
   When fever consumes the brain ?
Where is the hand that is hearty
   When pressure but drives a thorn ?
And who can enjoy a party
   Where one of the guests is Scorn ?

Pause then, and cease fault finding,
   For there lives not a faultless one ;

And love is a chain best binding
  The hearts by forbearance won ;
Tongues that are swift to censure
  The failings that all must share,
Will drive away those who venture
  Their fretful abuse to bear.
   *   *   *   *   *
Be not swift to find fault with one you love,
  Nor fretted at the failings of one that loves you ;
For joy would be banished from heaven above,
  If former sorrows were kept in view.

March 19, 1882.

To the Memory of John F. Darby.*

Sweet be thy rest, indomitable sage :
Let peace, well earned by toil, succeed old age.
Long life was thine ; and honors hard to gain
Lent joy to memory and pride to pain. -
Time was when men asked favors at thy hand,
And lavish Fortune heeded thy command ;
When on thy head there towered the leader's crest,
And ballots named thee better than the best.

---

*Last piece of poetry ever written by Col. Slayback.

Time was when Fate seemed powerless to kill,
And death stood hesitant before thy will.
Time was when glory and fair fortune fled,
And left thee battling for thy daily bread;
With crippled hands and torture-twisted feet,
The eye still blazed, the cheerful heart still beat,
And unrepining to thy daily task,
Without a murmur, or a boon to ask—
Time was when thou didst go, with scarce a friend
To heed thy struggles or thy words attend;
And yet thy life was greater at the last
Than when around thee Fortune's gifts were cast;
For in adversity thy dauntless soul
Rose like pure genius, bursting all control
Except its own strong will, and left behind
Proof that man has no master, save the mind.

St. Louis, May 15, 1882.

Stray Thoughts.

But unless the pent-up waters flow
  Stagnation makes them more impure ;
And griefs, which are unuttered, grow
  To suffering dire beyond a cure.

Of all the loves that ever were loved, this love was
  strongest and best ;
For it rose in the East with the rising sun, and went
  down with the sun in the West.

Not all the gold in all the ships
That ever sailed, on all the seas,
Could tempt me to live o'er again
The pangs of memory, keen with pain,
Since first I learned the power of love,
By losing first the power to please.

As through the darkly clouded sky
    Some rift reveals but one pale star,
So shines on me one faithful eye,
    Though darkness robes its beams afar.

Should scandal cloud the name I love,
    As dust may dim the diamond's ray,
Its value this shall not disprove,
    Or make me throw the gem away.

The sharp, keen struggle to forget
Hath cast oblivion over all the past,
Save those same scenes I would erase—
And efforts to expunge one face
Have shed dim mist o'er all, save that.

The choicest thoughts are often unexpressed,
The kindest words unsaid.

An awkward, unfortunate, blundering boy,
Always proud of bad luck, unaccustomed to joy,
He learned ere his time how to act like a man,
To resist any wrong and be true to his clan;
To pocket no slight and deserve no rebuff,
And to pity the rogue, when his foe cried "enough."

How pulse for pulse, and throb for throb,
    Our hearts concordant beat together;
Till fate our friendship's treasures rob,
    And force me from thee, dearest other.

He was a minstrel; in his mood
    Was wisdom mixed with folly;
A tame companion for the good,
But wild and fierce among the rude,
    And jovial with the jolly!

In man whom men condemn as ill
I find so much of goodness still;
    In man whom men pronounce divine
I find so much of sin and blot:
    I hesitate to draw the line
Between the two—since God has not.

Ah! who can tell how hard it is to climb
The steep where Fame's proud temple shines afar!
Ah! who can tell how many a soul sublime
Hath felt the influence of malignant star,
And waged with fortune an eternal war!

Tear one mortal more from earth,
Give one angel more its birth;
Dimmed and dull the sparkling eyes,
Till they flash in Paradise.

———

Tell me, best loved, and tell me true,
If I am best beloved by you?
For doubts are kin to pangs of death,
And doubting takes away my breath;
Then from my soul its anguish take,
And soothe my heart, or bid it break.

———

Last image on my heart ere sleep
   Its veil o'er memory throws,
And first when wakened senses leap
   To greet the dewy rose.

———

Not the lily fingered maid,
   Not the velvet bosomed lass,
Nurtured in domestic shade,
   Lives in marble or in brass;
Nor the plant that dares the storm
Can be sensitive in form.

The Missionary of the 19th Century.

His out-of-door smile for the stranger abroad,
  His every-day frown for his home ;
He has not a red for the poor in his road,
  But he pities the paupers—of Rome.

Those we Remember.

We'll not forget the smile of those
  Who never can forget our own ;
Nor those who gaze upon our woes
  With callous look or angry frown.

A Kiss.

When other lips on thine shall burn,
  Their second-handed fun I'll covet,
And wonder if they can discern
  The fire I left, and learn to love it.

Addresses.

Address at the Decoration of Soldiers' Graves,

Near St. Louis, May 30th, 1873.

Ladies and Gentlemen: When the feelings of the heart are touched, the utterances of the lips are imperfect. Bear with me then, my friends, to-day, if my words seem poorly chosen.

The grandeur and solemnity of this scene could borrow no impressiveness from displays of declamation, and figures of speech would impair the dignity of your own reflections.

This assemblage is only one of thousands like it throughout the United States, whose hands and thoughts are busy in decorating the resting-places of the gallant dead who perished in the late war.

But our observance of the day is distinguished
from the generality by a feature of rare and exquisite signification—a feature that is local now,
but destined, as we hope, to become national hereafter—a feature worthy of a place in history, as
a sign of the times in which we live, and of the
feelings which animate our community. It is this:

The Union soldiers and officers of St. Louis
having in charge the preparations for this cele-
bration, passed a resolution, prompted by their
own lofty and humane generosity, to the effect
that surviving Confederate soldiers be invited to
participate with them in the ceremonies of the
day, and that the graves of the soldiers who died
in the one cause should be decorated the same as
of those who fell for the other.

This beautiful and heroical action has met with
a response as sincere and spontaneous as the invitation was characteristic.

The Committee on Speakers have selected me,
as one who served the Confederacy during the
war, to deliver one of the addresses at Jefferson
Barracks, and, apprehensive as I was of my in-
ability to perform the exalted duty thus imposed,

I could not shrink from the responsibility. I come with you upon a pilgrimage of respect to the memory of brave men, who yielded up their lives to their honest convictions of duty.

We cannot approach this spot without feelings of deepest awe.

Jefferson Barracks is suggestive of important historical incidents of the war, and in this cemetery Union and Confederate soldiers slumber side by side, in the long, last sleep of death.

And here, about these sacred resting-places, are gathered the reconciled survivors, and the faithful and beautiful beings who love the soldier when living, and honor him when dead—the victors and the vanquished paying a mutual homage at the tomb of courage, and the fair hands and graceful forms of matron and maid dedicating the choicest offerings of spring at the shrine of valor.

O, my countrymen! what a spectacle is this! What a scene for the painter! What a theme for the poet! What a study for the historian of the future!

In the annals of human warfare, where can you find the record of any behavior more chivalrous and admirable than the conduct of the Union soldiers and officers of St. Louis in this affair?

It is true that from the most remote antiquity ceremonies similar to these have been celebrated by every cultured nation.

Flowers have had a delicate, universal language of their own, so ancient that its origin is lost in the fables of mythology.

But it has been reserved for the climax of Christian civilization, and the crowning illustration of American magnanimity, to make the floral pageantry of this day and hour the occasion for turning the wrath of enmity into praises, and the bitterness of mourning into the sweet uses of forgiveness and reconciliation.

The argument of superior force may sometimes be unanswerable. But to bring harmony out of discord requires a regard for the nobler and better feelings of our nature, and the exercise of the higher intellectual faculties.

When conciliation comes mingling with our reverence for the dead, it subdues the heart and propitiates the understanding.

And what nobler tribute could be paid the dead

than this, that not those alone who had been
friends, but those who had been adversaries too,
should come to do honor to the hero in his grave?
Not that our words can reach the sleeper. Ah! no,

" His blade leaps not at the long, loud cry,
Nor starts and streams with crimson dye;
He no more shouts ' Charge! ' nor the brave line leads,
For he sleeps in the grave of his glorious deeds."

But here, at a moment sacred to his memory,
those living can meditate upon the fleetingness
of life, look into each other's faces for compassion, and entreat that for all future time the
dwellers in our fair and bounteous land may be
brothers and friends, and countrymen, indeed.

It matters not, now, upon which side these
brave men contended. They were, and the war
has decided that they should ever remain, our
countrymen!

No bosom is so callous as to comprehend that
word and look upon their grave without compunction.

At the graves of those we venerate, our
thoughts peer deepest into immortality. The
fact that these still live in our affections is the

strongest proof we have that our own souls can never die. It is here we feel nearest to their actual presence.

And if the disembodied spirits of men are permitted to revisit their abodes on earth, it is not stretching the imagination far to see the shadowy hosts hovering over us to-day as we are assembled upon the hallowed ground where their bodies repose, and realize that they are influencing our thoughts and feelings with angelic inspiration.

O, gallant spirits! reproach us not that we have anticipated a pleasure of your calm existence by having ceased to hate on earth. We feel that what we do is prompted by your own heroic wishes. We lift our hands to you and invoke your co-operation. If you are gifted to guide the thoughts and actions of your survivors, let the purity of our motives in this our tribute at your shrine make us welcome, when our time shall come, to dwell in your starry regions.

Think not, my friends, that one of these has passed away in vain. In the economy of God, no death is premature where a human life is dedicated to an honest purpose.

But those of us who outlive them are respon-
sible for the use we make of the lesson of their
lives. In the olden time it was allotted to some
to perish in the wilderness—to others to reclaim
and beautify the promised land. It has been the
fate of these to die. It is ours for a little, a little, while to live.

We have not given the fatal proof of fidelity
to the cause we thought the right. We cannot
share the martyr wreaths they wear, but we can
honor their memory by leading stainless lives.
But it remains for us to make our devotion to the
welfare of our country as faithful, since it is denied us to make it as glorious, as theirs. And
God grant that when we come to take our places
with them we may not slumber in dishonored
graves.

Posterity will look—a generation already half-
grown since these brave men fell is already looking—to us for the moral and political import of
the war which convulsed this continent, and in
which we took part, some on one side and some
on the other.

Its results are not all known as yet. Far in the

future they will exert a powerful influence upon the destinies of our country.

But this we do know. That the modern prophets have been much at fault about the results thus far. Of these results none can be counted more remarkable than the tranquility the country has already reached. This has sorely perplexed the sages. Such a strife and such a pacification were never witnessed in the world before.

It is unprofitable to speculate about what might have been. It is wiser to recognize the irresistible logic of established events.

The war has demonstrated that no matter what construction the American citizen may place upon the Constitution, so jealously does he regard that instrument as the only safeguard of the liberties of his country, that rather than submit to what he considers an infringement upon its provisions, he is ready to die.

The love of constitutional liberty is his grand ruling passion.

It is apparent that outside of a few heartless agitators each party was sincere in the belief that the other party was inimical to the principles of the Constitution.

It was this devotion to Constitutional liberty, as the respective sections had been educated to regard it, that impelled each party to the dreadful onset, and it was this same principle that made peace possible after the sanguinary encounter was over.

It may be that wise statesmanship could and should have averted the conflict. But it was not done, and we can only deal with the facts as we find them. In the settlement of complicated difficulties, it is sometimes necessary for States as for individuals to have a fight before they can come to a satisfactory and peaceful understanding.

In just such a complication the sections of this country were involved in 1861, and it, perhaps, was incumbent upon the men of that day to fight. But now that the controversy is over, it is not incumbent on us to keep up enmity. Two knights once disputed as to the color of a shield. One said it was blue; the other said it was green. The code was appealed to and both were mortally wounded. Then the by-standers discovered that both were right, and both were wrong. The shield had been suspended between them. One side was painted blue; the other, green. Each had stated correctly the side he had seen, and of course had misstated the side he had not seen.

Missourians have just cause for State pride in seeing their sons step forward in initiating complete fellow-citizenship. There is no valid reason why it should be deferred.

The Missouri troops, on both sides, were distinguished for being the foremost soldiers in battle, and they can afford to let those who did not gain any distinction in the field quarrel now.

Missourians are done with that, and are going on now at something else. Life is too short. They have no time to waste. The present urges. The future beckons. They have something better to do than to cherish revenge. They cannot recall the past. They cannot bring back the dead. They cannot be enemies, and, since they have determined to be countrymen, they have resolved to be friends.

This day decides that resentment shall not mar the future of our beloved country.

In 1865, the enemies of our institutions abroad made sage predictions that the banner of the Southern Cross was only furled for a time; but our own poet said that it was furled forever.

Toward the close of the war there was a deeper dread in the mind of the Southern soldier than his customary encounter of superior numbers of armed men. It was not that he stood one of eight millions facing thirty millions that caused him to succumb; it was not that he felt unwilling to starve and go ragged; it was not that his faith was shaken in his generals; and it was not the ships, the money, the iron or the splendid munitions of war arrayed against him that reconciled him to abandon the unequal contest in which he had so often and so freely hazarded his life.

It was not that he had forgotten his provocations, or underrated them, and it was not that he was a traitor to his cause.

Then why did he surrender? you will ask. My friends, I will tell you why: and this day and hour presents the first fitting opportunity for a true Southern man to make such a disclosure without having his language or his motives misconstrued.

I will tell you why the Southern soldiers grew weary of the contest and surrendered their arms. It was because, after all their privations and losses, and cruel grief over the bloody graves of their fallen comrades, they began to look to the future, and to say: " Well, what then ? "

Made wiser by the stern education of war, their love of constitutional liberty made them tremble for the consequences of final success. They saw that the end of the war in that way would be but the beginning of others.

They cast their eyes upon the government at Richmond, and its constitution recognizing the right of any State in certain contingencies to set up a separate nationality for itself, with its little President and its little Senate, its little Supreme Court and its little Navy, with its Palmetto, its Pelican, or its Lone Star for its flag, and the soldier began to ask himself, " For what am I fighting? Will my children be better off when the wrongs I am redressing shall have been succeeded by others of greater magnitude? Will my constitutional rights that will remain to me in either event be as safe under the new nationality as under the old? And what can posterity gain by exchanging for still another experiment the illustrious fabric that Washington, Hamilton, Jefferson and Adams, and the brave, wise and good men who shared their counsels and their dangers, established and bought with the blood of my ancestry of the revolution of 1776?"

It was this appalling logic which fastened upon the minds of the Southern soldiers

    " Like a phantasm, or a hideous dream; "

and then, and not until then, did their hearts begin to fail them.

Hence it was that when they furled their flag they furled it forever.

Hence it was that when they laid down their arms they did so with the full expectation, wish and understanding that the flag they had fought should become the emblem of their chosen nationality, and that from thenceforth and forever these States should be in fact, as in name, THE UNITED STATES OF AMERICA.

And hence it was that when the Southern

soldiers gave up, they surrendered in just as dead earnest as they had fought.

The generalship, the courage, the patience, fidelity and fortitude of the Southern army awakened the wonder and admiration of the world. They had performed prodigies of valor, and these prodigies the Federal soldier had overcome. The magnificent energy of the struggle was at an end, and the country had stood the test of a general civil war. The war was over. But there yet remained the problem of pacification. Could such armies be disbanded without the destruction of social order?

Would those who had won let victory suffice? Would those who had lost resort to guerrilla warfare? Would there have to be maintained a standing army in every city, a garrison in every village, to hunt down human tigers in every thicket, swamp and mountain?

Was there to be a gibbet in every churchyard, and bushwhackers in the tangled breaks of every river bank?

The question was of profound concern to everybody. It had to be decided, then and there.

A mistake would have been fatal; delay, impossible. It was a critical moment.

The spirit of American civilization is broad and generous. The very air we breathe is electric with magnanimity. The strength to overcome brave men in battle is stimulated by a heroism that scorns to strike down an unarmed foe. But beyond any of these considerations, the American soldier was swayed by a sense of political duty, and in this trying crisis, once more DEVOTION TO THE PRINCIPLES OF CONSTITUTIONAL LIBERTY lifted him above the passions and madness of the hour.

The surrender had been unconditional. But history will record that the conditions exacted were as honorable to those who imposed as to those who accepted them.

The treatment of General Lee by General Grant at Appomattox, and of General Joseph E. Johnston by General Sherman at Durham Station, shed a lustre upon those great leaders that will only brighten with the lapse of time.

And on the other hand the conduct of General Lee and General Johnston from that time forward excelled all praise.

But it was the whole-souled character of the soldiers themselves that carried into practice the illustrious examples of their commanders.

Since the war the victors have conducted themselves with moderation—the vanquished with manliness.

On the one hand there has been clemency and forbearance akin to sympathy. On the other, acquiescence in the new order of things, and an honest endeavor to repair the damages of the war.

The sword of the stronger, flushed with victory, has been sheathed in its scabbard. The hand of the weaker has not reached out for the sword of which it has been disarmed. The one has disdained advantage. The other has detested revenge. The one has been tenderly generous. The other has been proudly grateful.

It would be hard to say why such men should not forgive each other. Animosity can only mar the happiness of both, and narrow indeed must be the soul which could desire to keep it up. When Rome's immortal orator was reproached for defending a former enemy, he exclaimed:

"*Neque me vero poenitet mortales inimicitias sempiternas amicitias habere.*" And why should not we too boast that our enmities are mortal as the garlands that we bring, and our friendships as enduring as the grave that they adorn.

Empires rise, flourish, crumble and decay. The marble of the new is exhumed from the ruins of the old. The destiny of nations is guided by a Power above and beyond the will of man. They are born, grow old and die as individuals by an inscrutable law ordained by the All-wise Lawgiver of the Universe. For some reason beyond our search, mankind have always been at war; and while the laws governing human nature remain the same, wars will go on until the millenium. The war-making capacity of a nation determines its rank among the nations of the world, and the military genius of its people is a test of its durability. The individual must be willing to perish that his nationality, through his devotedness, may live on. And no first-class power has ever yet existed so supreme that it could afford to alienate the affections or disregard the rights of any considerable number of its citizens.

And, my friends, just as long as our country remains liable at any time to become involved in war, we owe it to ourselves and our children to preserve the good-will of the soldiers of the republic towards our beloved institutions, and stimulate their devotion to constitutional liberty. And who are now our soldiers? Are they confined to a section? • Are they embraced in a creed? Do they belong to a class? No! The army that keeps the outside world in awe is composed of all citizens capable of bearing arms, of all sections, political parties and antecedents. The stalwart and valiant men who are now busy everywhere plying the forge, holding the plow, pushing the industries of every section, and region and State—a self-sustaining host, governing themselves, and capable of defending that government against the combined world in arms—these constitute the true grand army of the republic. And God grant that civil strife may never again darken and desolate our homes; that, whenever duty calls upon the citizens of the United States to repel invasion or vindicate the national honor, no grievances may lurk behind us, but may we all be found side by side in the lists of glory, battling for the sacred principle of constitutional liberty.

Oh, priceless boon! purchased at inestimable cost! For this the men we commemorate to-day have died. They died that we might live in peace, contentment and good-will. Let us hal'ow their dust. Let us honor their courage. Let us venerate their motives. Let us cherish their memory!

WOMANLY AMBITION.

An Address before the Young Ladies' Literary Society of Lindenwood Female College, St. Charles, Mo., June 3, 1875.

Love of glory is the universal passion of mankind. It is the actuating principle in every grand achievement, and in a modified degree it prompts the lowly as it stirs the great.

The desire of power and influence, the love of praise, the struggle for eminence, the emulation to out-do others, that honor and distinction among men may follow, may all be summed up in one word, ambition.

The effect of this passion upon individual life and character is of infinite diversity, and varies with the innate disposition and external circumstances of every human being. Action and motive are often discordant. Persons intend one thing, and find they have done another ; desire one fate, and have to accept another. And yet for all this, the soul that is resolute performs so many exploits that savor of impossibility, that those who wish to do something grand in the world find more force in what they wish than what they know. The wishes of the heart put brain and hand to work. The intellect is dormant until the feelings call its contriving powers into exercise. Thought succeeds to impulse. Action follows thought. Results follow action. Success smiles only on persistent toil and vigilance. Thus is the record made up of human achievement, and thus the cherished ambition of any life goes far to shape its career and fix its destiny.

When ambition springs from proper motives, it is laudable, and stimulates all the faculties to their loftiest energy. When it emanates from selfish greed for advantage over others, it is satanic. The one is true; the other, false. The one has been said to raise mortals to the skies. The other to drag angels down.

Ambition, in its charitable sense, is consistent with every womanly attribute.

The wish to attain excellence, the desire to confer blessings and to earn gratitude, the holy aspiration to be goodly great and greatly good, are the noblest incentives that can actuate a soul. These incentives have belonged to women, as to men, ever since the world began, and will so continue as long as the world may last. Side by side in the lists of the truly great, the names of illustrious women vie with those of distinguished men, both in war and peace. In statesmanship, diplomacy, philosophy, literature, science and art—as ruler, as teacher, as poet—in all the loftier planes of intellectual attainment, women of genius have left as enduring monuments of greatness as the men. In our own day, the sculptor, the author, the orator, and the king, win no fairer renown than the sculptress, the authoress, the oratress, and the queen. It is, therefore, fair to assume that, in intellect, woman is the equal of

man, and if there are distinctions between manly
and womanly ambition, they consist rather in the
quality than in the quantity of characteristic
force.

Men love power for the sake of dominion;
women for the sake of splendor. Men demand
obedience; women admiration. Men seize the
sword; women the scepter. Men conquer that
they may rule; women that they may reign.
Man is ambitious to give battle; woman to be
supreme in the hearts of her people. Men like
to be formidable abroad; women to be beloved
at home. Men fight for fame; women shrink from
reproach. Men glory in their strength; women
in their delicacy and refinement. Men study self-
promotion; women the promotion of those they
love. Man's ambition is to subdue; woman's to
please. Man's ambition revels in the triumphs
of the world; but the ambition of a true woman
is consecrated to God.

Semiramis leading the Assyrian hosts; Zenobia
at the head of her army, making armed protest
against the ruin of her beloved Palmyra by the
mailed legions of Rome; Joan d'Arc inspiring

the drooping defenders of France against the victorious English; and Marie Antoinette enduring the awful terrors of execution with sublime fortitude, are historical instances among thousands that could be named, to prove that women are as exalted in their courage and their heroism as men.

Every-day life points to the same conclusion. The statistics of the census show that where numbers are about equal, women possess more moral courage and fortitude than men. Man pleads, as his excuse for intemperance and crime, that he is poor, that he is wretched, that he is tempted. But woman, equally poor, equally wretched, equally tempted, resists the temptation, and does not yield to intemperance and crime.

The police reports show the cringing slaves of intemperance are mostly men. The criminal records show that nearly all the criminals are men. Intellectually man's equal, morally his superior, woman's ambition is purer, nobler, and more truly heroic.

There are occasions when to be patient is to be great; to be silent is to be heroic; to be uncomplaining partakes of the sublime. It is on such occasions that the average woman is superior to the average man, and that the truly great women furnish evidences of character so exalted that they seem to rise above the human, and to be angelic in their natures. There may be, therefore, a womanly ambition to excel in those admirable characteristics which are beyond the capabilities of man, and in which she is by nature his superior. On the other hand, there are many things right enough in themselves which a woman of refinement cannot engage in without compromising her sense of delicacy. A true woman has an innate modesty that holds in subjection every wish of her heart. Men may seek notoriety as the prelude to more enduring fame. A woman cannot do this, and with sublime resignation many a woman, who knows within her soul that she is great, shrinks from celebrity and lives for those she loves. Nay, more—she is content to let them wear the bays that might have crowned her own brow. Many a man achieves fortune through the sound sense of his wife. Many a man has been illustrious on brain-capital furnished by a woman. But for

Aspasia, Pericles would never have established that republic of letters which gave to Greece its golden age; but for Isabella, Columbus would never have discovered America; but for Malinchi, Cortez would never have conquered Mexico; but for Miss Dent, Ulysses Grant would never have been President of the United States. Almost every illustrious man who ever lived became distinguished by following the advice of some sensible woman, and many of these same men fell from their highest estate by sinning against her better judgment and purer intellectuality.

Woe be to the man who dares to trample her under his feet!

Alexander the Great, Tarquin, Julius Cæsar, Napoleon and Byron are examples of warning to mankind that the greatest cannot escape destruction if they sin against woman's better promptings or reject her counsel. And our own beloved Washington points the moral of maintaining a proper deference for her true worth and intellectual power; and in nearly every household in the land the sweet, placid face of Martha Washington smiles from the same wall along with the Father of his Country. She never dreamed of such renown as this, but did her duty, and gave her advice and managed her estate in good womanly fashion for the sake of a better reward than fame—the approval of her own conscience, the advancement of her husband's interests, and the hope of that eternal crown reserved for the chosen of God.

Women are often ambitious to have influence in directions that render them unhappy. They wish to be lawyers and doctors, and preachers and newspaper reporters, etc. Some of them do very well, too. But in aspiring to eminence in such pursuits, a woman throws away her chances of best success, and gives up her greatest power. She is heiress to the crown in the social kingdom. Her highest supremacy can be reached in those fields of usefulness which tend to make homes happy. There is no such thing as a paradise on earth without a pure, good woman as its ruling spirit—its gentle law-giver, regulating its peace by the wonderful harmonies of love and sympathy.

There are a great many little kingdoms called homes. Unless they are governed by the power of woman's rule, they are dreary places. Without her taste, her care, her skill, palaces and cottages are but miserable under whatever government man can devise.

It is woman's proud office to govern and sanctify home, and to make its influence sacred.

The young and the aged look to her gentle hand for tenderness, and the strong and the weary look to her for rest. Instinctively she loves truth. Naturally she recoils from dishonor, and by tradition she preserves the fidelity, the honest pride and the priceless decencies of the family fireside.

There is no field for womanly ambition so suited to her natural genius as excellence in domestic pursuits.

> "Honor and fame from no condition rise;
> Act well your part—there all the honor lies."

Ambition, to be wholesome in its effects, should be within bounds and conformable to the situation and circumstances of the individual. It must be directed in channels of common sense and possibility. Not only mental, but physical, endowments must be taken into account. Persons capable of attaining distinction as poets might fail as mechanics. The accidents of birth, station, property, relationship to others, and the times in which one lives, must all be reconcilable with the object to be accomplished.

In reading the story of any remarkable life, what little things seem to have occasioned the great ones! Through what years of patient obscurity most of the famous were disciplined!

> Ah! who can tell how hard it is to climb
> The steep where Fame's proud temple shines afar?
> Ah! who can tell how many a soul sublime
> Hath felt the influence of malignant star,
> And waged with Fortune an eternal war?

Sometimes persons are great in one direction, and ambitious in another. Sound judgment should always be consulted, or ambition becomes ridiculous. It would be out of place for a woman to be a blacksmith or a stage driver. A woman's ambition should prompt her to endeavor to excel in those things for which she is adapted. I have seen a little girl put on her mother's dress, and peep over her shoulder to see how she looked wearing a train. Some grown-up persons are as absurd as this little child in fun. A woman has to consider not only what she can do, but what would be proper and becoming for her to do. She should never lose her good taste. It is therefore most important for a woman who has ambition not to mistake her work.

This brings us to consider, what is womanly work? The question is sometimes right difficult to answer. It depends a good deal on circumstances. It may become necessary, in the life of any woman, to earn an honest living in the world. Too little attention is paid by parents and educators to this important contingency.

It is too often taken for granted, that if a girl be fair, winsome, and intelligent, she need never trouble herself about it. And yet it is worthy her most serious consideration. It is the fashion for mothers to have a false, pernicious ambition for their daughters to have worthless hands and haughty hearts; bent upon making display in what is called the best society, and repel the thought that these girls ever had to depend upon themselves. It is a cruel wrong, this false ambition of mothers. Cruel to themselves, and still more cruel to their daughters. True ambition and true kindness alike dictate that every girl, no matter what her station, should be carefully instructed in some useful industry for which there is a market demand, and by which an honest support can be made. I hesitate to lift the veil of reality to bright young eyes before me. But scarcely a day passes in the office of any business man in our large cities that some young lady does not come with lamentations that she has been compelled by changes in the fortunes of those she depended upon to go forth in the world to struggle for subsistence. She is told to teach school. "Alas! sir, I am not thorough enough in anything to teach. I cannot get a situation over graduates of the Normal School." She is told to sew. "Alas! I have never been taught to sew; I cannot even make my own dresses. I cannot compete with girls trained to sew, and they almost starve at it." She is told to learn millinery. "Alas! to learn that requires time and money, and I have neither. Apprentices are not paid

even their board." She is told to copy manu-
scripts. "Alas! there is no bread in that. What
little there is in that line is absorbed by expert
penmen who work rather for employment than
for pay." She is told to seek a situation as a
nurse or house-girl. "Sir, I have been tenderly
raised. Raised as a lady, and the equal of any
one. I cannot consent to be reduced to servitude."

And the misguided ambition of the mother
shines through eyes that are full of tears—tears
of agony, tears that would never have flowed if
the mother had done her duty and taught the
girl to work.

So this girl—educated, as the fashion goes; accomplished, as it is falsely called; worthless, in
fact, for the grand mission of self-preservation,
comes to grief and must seek refuge in a distaste-
ful marriage, or humiliating dependence upon
those to whom she is a burden.

True ambition would raise every girl so as to
make an independent support for herself, if
necessity should demand it. Nay, more, to direct
her energies in some useful occupation that will
enlist her mind as well as her hand, circumscribe

her leisure hours, absorb her time, limit her wishes, keep her out of mischief and aloof from temptation.

It is a crying evil and a shame in this country that girls should not be better prepared for changes of fortune by being taught to work ; and not merely taught to work, but trained to work at something that will earn bread.

This may be plain, perhaps unpleasant, talk, but there are few very secure fortunes in this country, and I have seen the daughter of a millionaire reduced to poverty, deserted by her husband for no fault of hers, living upon the charity of her former slaves.

When such transmutations are possible, what security is there for the daughters of aristocrats, worth from five to ten thousand dollars? Every sign in nature, every voice within us, every wise teaching that come to us from without, admonish us that earth is but a colony, and that usefulness in some industry is the condition upon which a settler is received, and the idle are but burthens whose room would be better than their company.

This is a topic that is spoken of oftener in a

whisper in the family circle than in polite society. But a woman does not like to be under pecuniary obligations and her sensitive nature scorns debt. It is a great pity that our customs and conventionalities do not provide more ways for the remunerative employment of women who are ambitious to earn an honest living ; for, be assured, this, too, is a womanly ambition.

There is need and there is room for hard thinking and practical invention on this subject of work that will pay, and work that women can do without being ashamed of ridicule, or at the risk of endangering the health.

Besides, the errors prevalent about womanly work, our customs and conventionalities occasion other false ambitions. To be the belle of a ball; to lead the fashion; to put on style in dress ; to marry a count, or some other nobody, with a large foreign title ; to be considered beautiful; to excite the envy of the other girls and cut them out in the admiration of their sweet-hearts; to display extravagant jewelry ; to go around collecting money in little ridiculous sums to get a reputation as alms-givers by making others contribute to charities that they do not like to give to themselves; to belong to the lobby of Congress, or the Legislature—all these are morbid, false, unwomanly ambitions, that lead to bitterness and sorrow.

They are beneath the ambition of a true woman, and unworthy of a wise one, who chooses, like Mary, " the better part."

What is worth living for? What is worth dying for? These are the questions that underlie all human endeavor. Make up your mind in answer to these, and you will know what existence is worth.

A woman's life can be exalted and sublime in itself, without being made conspicuous in the world. It is not only her province to be truly great, but to be the inspiring cause of true greatness in others. She is the natural teacher of the world. Hers are the moral forces; it is hers to suggest grand ideas; it is hers to rebuke exalted error; it is hers to sanction or to condemn the elaborate evolutions of man's mental exertion. Her quiet judgment is more decisive than debate; her persistent disapprobation is often more dreadful than battle. Napoleon could overthrow the veteran legions of armed Europe, but he could not endure the refined criticism of Madame de Stael.

Skeptics may cavil and infidels croak, but as the mothers in the land find peace, comfort and refuge in the consolations of religion, its teachings and its blessings will sanctify the homes and hearts of the faithful. Armies cannot crush, argument cannot shake, the doctrines that she teaches to the children at her knee. Trial, persecution, martyrdom look into her faithful face, and renew their trust in God.

> "Not she with traitorous lips the Master stung;
> Not she betrayed him with unfaithful tongue.
> She, when apostles fled, could danger brave;
> Last at the cross, and earliest at the grave."

Her fidelity is truer than man's. Her pure affection only ends with life.

There is nothing in all literature more characteristic of woman, or more touching, than Ruth's reply to Naomi: "Entreat me not to leave thee, or to return from following after thee, for whither thou goest I will go, and where thou lodgest I will lodge; thy people shall be my people, and thy God my God. Where thou diest I will die, and there will I be buried."

A true woman does good for its own sake, and wishes as little said about it as possible. She would rather die in obscurity than to have fame throughout the world, coupled with fame's twin sister—calumny. It is within her province to study those things which bless and benefit others.

Through patriotism for her people, Esther periled her life and her position ; and every-day life brings into observation the self-denying, self-sacrificing devotion of woman, struggling with heroic disregard to censure or applause, to promote the welfare of others.

Scarcely a day passes in any life that the judgment of each individual is not called upon to decide in the conflict between inclination and duty. You are to choose and to decide—to decide and to persevere—to persevere and to conquer, or to surrender and die. If the wishes of the heart are kept right, the will to do or to suffer for the sake of right must triumph. What you wish to do becomes your ambition just as soon as you are in earnest. You can only be in earnest when you feel your secret thoughts and wishes are inspired by resignation to the will of God. Would you be truly great, cultivate thoughts and wishes that are ennobling. Would you be truly good, look to the Divine source of all goodness.

"Whatsoever things are true; whatsoever things are just; whatsoever things are pure; whatsoever things are lovely; whatsoever things are of good report; if there be any virtue, and if there be any praise, think on these things."

To build up pleasant places along the paths of life; to soothe the brow of pain; to watch the bedside of the sick; whisper words of sympathy to troubled hearts; to inspire with hope and courage the weak and weary victims of despair; to point with hands angelic to the mercy-seat of God, and, in the unobtrusive spirit of the Great Master, to win back the erring and the wayward to a sense of duty; to purify the conscience and exalt the purposes of the young: these things are great. Life cannot be dedicated to nobler aspirations, death cannot close upon sublimer career. And yet they are all consistent with womanly ambition.

LEAGUED LAWYERS.

The Colorado State Bar Association Formed. Address by Col. Slayback, of St. Louis, at Denver, Sept. 11th, 1882.

The members of the legal profession of Colorado met for the purpose of forming a state bar association in the United States, with an attendance of about 150 of the leading lawyers of the state.

Col. A. W. Slayback, of St. Louis, who had been invited to be present and deliver an address, was then introduced by the chair and spoke as follows:

MR. CHAIRMAN AND GENTLEMEN OF THE COLORADO BAR: I have lingered beyond the time contemplated for my return to my distant home, that I might not seem unmindful of the distinguished honor conferred by the invitation to address you upon the occasion of your convention, for the purpose of forming a state bar association.

The object for which you are assembled is one which naturally enlists the cordial co-operation of every one who holds in reverence the higher aims and purposes of your profession. Lawyers devote their lives to the advocacy of human rights, and to the proper administration of justice.

They study books and study men. They investigate science itself, and thrust the probe of disputation into the very vitals of philosophy in order that truth may live and error die.

The discipline of their profession tends to enlarged and constantly enlarging charity. They know what it is for the best of friends to maintain different opinions upon an agreed state of facts. They know what it is to see their deepest and most earnest convictions overruled by the solemn judgment of courts, whose honesty of purpose cannot be questioned, and again, where their own doubts prevail, they find, after careful argument, that the actual right is where they first surmised a wrong. The legislature frames a law;

the courts expound it; but the lawyers must see
that the law, so made and expounded, is prop-
erly applicable to the facts of each particular
case. Differences of opinion arise—honest differences. It is not true that lawyers see a thing
as they are paid to see it. It is the mission of
the true lawyer to settle controversies, not to
foster them. But when controversies have arisen
they should be determined according to the eternal principles of truth and justice, and in ascertaining the correct application of those principles
there should be the greatest latitude of free discussion and the total banishment of all personal
animosity.

A proper respect for the law is best engendered
among the people whenever they see all the
officers of the courts conducting themselves with
decorum and integrity.

Instead of regarding the practice of law as a
system of cunning tricks and devices, the true
advocate beholds in it the majesty and benevo-
lence of peace and order; protection against ruf-
fianly violence; the shelter of the weak against
the strong; the checking of craftiness and fraud

upon the unwary or the helpless; the assertion of that pure type of liberty which deprives no man of his property or his pleasure so long as he inflicts no damage upon society or the individuals who compose society; and the adjustment and distribution of property and privilege so that no man shall suffer in his feelings, or lose that which is his own without obtaining prompt and adequate redress.

What moral and physical courage is required to make a man, who is trained to please if he can, stand up for the rights of a client, or the cause he deems proper, while the public sentiment is all against him! It is some strength to the champion of justice at such an hour to feel that he has the respect, the confidence and the sympathy of his manly professional brethren.

Bar associations are designed to cultivate fraternal feelings among honorable members, the men who are imbued with the philosophy and alive to the dignity of the legal profession, and to elevate the standard of ethics.

Lawyers are often hated unjustly for espousing a cause which has but few friends, but it becomes their duty to see that the law is administered without fear, favor or affection, regardless of popular clamor, and independent of personal feelings.

The bar association is a strength and refuge to the honorable man and it is a dread to the evildoer.

No saint ever wore a robe that some demon would not steal to serve the devil in, and of course a bad man will now and then gain admittance to the bar. But take them numerically as compared with other callings and professions and the average standard of honor and integrity is as high, if not higher, in the legal profession than in any other. I will make no exception. And the jokes and gibes at lawyers' expense, and the caricatures made of them by witless dramatists to please ignorant and vicious auditories, while generally treated as beneath all notice by lawyers, are nevertheless aimed at a very limited portion of the profession whose members it is the mission of the bar association to weed out.

Those of you who have belonged to such organizations in older states have witnessed their beneficial influence, not only upon the bar, but upon the whole entire community.

The bar association is an adjunct of advanced civilization, educating the conscience of the profession and drawing a line between the regulars and the guerrillas in the great army of law and order.

In a country where government itself simply means the supremacy of law, rather than the will or the opinion of any individual, whatever has a tendency to elevate, enlighten and advance the character of the legal profession, exalts the standard of civilization and benefits the entire community.

In a progressive age, and a prosperous and progressive country erroneous judgment can no longer mark injustice with the exploded sanction of authority. It is the axiom of modern learning that law is discovered, not made, and decisions have weight, not according to their antiquity, but in proportion as they conform to correct reasoning and sound sense.

Jurisprudence constitutes so important a part in human affairs that whatever men find worth struggling for, must rank in secondary and subordinate position to the paramount consideration of establishing corrrect principles for the assertion and maintenance of human rights, and the redress and punishment for human wrongs. For the security of life, property and peace of mind the people must often look to their lawyers.

Confidence must be reposed; property must be entrusted; responsibilities must be lodged in the lawyer. If he proves unfaithful or treacherous, scarcely any punishment is considered too severe for him; but there is one punishment he is always sure to get, and that, too, not easy to be borne, and that is the united scorn and contempt of all the honorable members of the profession. And there is no possible solace in any transient advantage that can compensate an apostate practitioner for bringing that sort of disgrace upon himself which will not fade or wash out.

Whatever lends dignity to the court and its officers carries dread to the breast of the wrongdoer. Whatever lessens the estimate in which lawyers are held impedes the administration of justice; and the estimate lawyers entertain for each other is apt to extend to the community outside. They are presumed, like brothers, to know each other, and I venture to assert that no man can rise to distinction and success at the American bar, in any of the states, unless he passes through that straight and narrow gateway—the recognition and indorsement of his brother lawyers. It may come slowly, reluctantly; but it must and will come, if by his conduct, bearing, learning and industry the practitioner secures the good will and the applause of his professional brethren.

Hence the importance of cultivating those amenities, courtesies and decencies of debate which, amid the conflicts of interests and the collision of intellects, do not detract from the force of an argument or the scope of true reason, and yet impart sweetness and serenity to the labors and disappointments, the heart-aches and the anxieties of a lawyer's life.

The rivalries and contentions of lawyers often give them the appearance of gladiators pitted against each other for the mere purpose of affording savage satisfaction to their spectators by reason of the punishment and pain they inflict upon each other. To the zealous advocate, alive to his client's interest and cause, this is a tempting trap. But it is a fatal trap for the peace and prosperity of the profession. There should be some influence hanging, ever overhanging us, to remind us that our opponent in the argument is personally a brother and a friend, whose sympathies and sufferings, labors and fellowship should not be sacrificed on the foul altar of false advantage.

The bar association tends to refine the social pleasures and to soothe the angry impulses, and affords a sort of *locus penitentiæ* for good fellows to make friends again after they have been temporarily angry with and enstranged from each other. Its influence is at once elevating and comforting, and those who stand aloof from such organizations are not full and well-rounded men, but are somewhere deficient.

Although Missouri has been a state for about fifty-two years, our bar association is only going on two years old. The St. Louis bar association was organized several years before that of the state, and was found to work so well that the lawyers throughout the state were encouraged to establish a co-operative and more general organization. The effect and influence of the St. Louis bar association upon the legislature of the state have been marked and gratifying.

The statutes relating to civil practice and to a large number of important topics have been improved and corrected by bills drawn by our committee, discussed, matured and recommended by the association, and whenever the legislature for want of time or for want of intelligence neglected to heed the suggestions of the association, we always had the satisfaction to believe the legislature was wrong.

The promoting of social relations and good feeling among the members has also marked the history of our association, and I cordially congratulate the members of the profession in your magnificent young state, where everything seems new except your civilization, upon securing for yourself the advantages of such an association.

You have done that within six years which it took other states fifty to accomplish. Colorado owes much of its rapid development to the sage counsel, the brilliant abilities and the progressive spirit of her bar. Colossal fortunes have grown up under their advice. Many of them were distinguished in other states before they drifted here for health, or business, and among the number, if you will excuse a personal allusion which is not invidious, there is one *nomo probus et integer*—who, standing at the head of a noted bar in Missouri, with the generosity of a prince and the wisdom of a sage, directed the law studies and gave a helping hand to many a young man struggling for admission to the bar, and, among them, to one who comes to-day from a distant home, that he may return to him and thank him.

The Study of Nature and The Study of Art.

Two Addresses Delivered at the Annual Commencement of the Missouri School of Mines and Metallurgy, at Rolla, Mo., June 12th, 1879, and June 9th, 1881, respectively.

THE STUDY OF NATURE.

All thought is precious; all study is valuable; all learning is useful; all knowledge leads to further knowledge; all science exalts and ennobles the understanding; but the grand total of all thought, study, learning, knowledge and science is reached when the human mind becomes enabled to cast one rational, intelligent glance upon the Universe as a whole.

There shine the flaming suns; there roll the countless planets; there space invites to space still more profound; there comets in eccentric orbits range; there light, heat, force and motion play with the mighty spheres as toys; and through and throughout all this magnificent array of wonders we discern that law prevails—order, harmony, system, plan, *design*. Educated reason recognizes these evidences of contrivance, and knows that somewhere there is a Lawgiver, a Contriver, a Ruler, as supreme and infinite as the displays of His works are sublime and beautiful.

Speculations upon the origin of matter, the duration of it, the destiny and final disposition awaiting it, are interesting, and furnish the occasion for noting and preserving observations of particular facts.

But the power to reason from special facts to general laws must often stop there. The re-application of those general laws to other facts not submitted to our observations must involve us at once in conjecture and uncertainty—mere guess work at best. But there are things we *can* know which concern us much more vitally, and these it is given us to know with certainty, and to establish by actual demonstration beyond contradiction or question.

Humboldt has remarked: "The aspect of external nature, as it presents itself in its generality to thoughtful contemplation, is that of unity in diversity, and of connection, resemblance and order, among created things most dissimilar in their form: one fair, harmonious whole.

"To seize this unity and this harmony amid such an immense assemblage of objects and forces; to embrace alike the discoveries of the earliest ages and those of our own time, and to analyze the details of phenomena without sinking under their mass, are efforts of human reason in the path wherein it is given to man to press towards the full comprehension of nature, to unveil a portion of her secrets, and by the force

of thought to subject to his intellectual dominion
the rough materials which he collects by observation."

Nearly all of the errors which have at different
eras become prevalent among mankind have
been occasioned by a partial or imperfect observation of facts.

It amazes us now that whole armies of brave
men should have fallen into consternation because of an eclipse of the sun, or the appearance
of a comet, or the flash of a meteor.

Ignorance of the laws of nature has caused
men to impute every operation of natural force
to the malign influence of some pagan deity, and
it was only in comparatively modern times that
prolonged attention to facts, about which there
could arise no dispute, led to the disclosure and
demonstration of those mighty truths which
exist under the surface of things, and which
escape superficial observation.

The slowness of men in arriving at these great
truths has also been retarded by superstition,
prejudice, bigotry and persecution—fetters to
progress, which, happily for our race, are grad-

ually relaxing their hold upon the republic of thinkers.

The influence of education for good or evil is shown in nothing stronger than in this.

It was oftentimes more difficult to make the truth believed than to find it. Men would insist upon thinking as they had been taught to think.

It is recorded that when Alexander captured Babylon, Aristotle, who was his tutor, received from Calisthenes, a Chaldean astronomer, a catalogue of eclipses observed at the temple of Belus during a previous period of 1903 years. The ancient Egyptians were also versed in astronomical study at a remote antiquity. The valuable writings and observations of Hipparchus, who lived about two centuries before Christ, nearly all perished with the destruction of the Alexandrian library ; but Ptolemy, having rescued one book, made it the foundation of studies during the reigns of the Emperors Adrian and Antoninus, which resulted in the enunciation by him of the system known as the Ptolemaic.

According to it, the earth was spherical, but supposed to be the immovable centre of the

Universe. The sun, moon, planets and fixed stars were supposed to revolve around it, in perfect circles, and with uniform velocities, in accordance with the appearance of the Universe at first glance to the physical eye. This was substantially the opinion of that master mind of all the Greeks, Aristotle, who was the greatest original thinker the world has ever produced.

This doctrine remained unshaken until less than four hundred years ago. Nicolaus Copernicus was born in 1473. He received a classical and scientific education at the University of Cracow, and finished his studies in Italy. He taught mathematics at Rome, and returned to Prussia to become Canon of Frauenburg. He was a teacher, a physician and a priest. He surpassed the mathematicians of his time in the diligence of his studies, before he turned his principal attention to astronomy. At the close of his seventy years of laborious life his works were published, and the notions of Aristotle and Hipparchus and Ptolemy were exploded.

The Copernican system, as it is called, may be briefly described as follows:

That the sun and stars are stationary; the moon only revolves about the earth; the earth is a planet whose orbit is between Venus and Mars; the planets revolve about the sun, and the apparent revolution of the heavens is caused by the rotation of the earth on its axis.

It is a remarkable fact, that the first copy of his works was placed in his hands the very day of his death.

But astronomer like, he had gazed on nature with a lover's eye—pondered over the records of previous observers—left his own record for those who were to come after him, and at his allotted threescore years and ten succumbed to fate, bequeathing to his followers the glorious fruits of his life-long studies.   He died in 1543.

About the year 1608, two rival spectacle makers of Middleburg, Hans Lippersheim and Jacob Adrianz, claimed each the invention of the instrument called the telescope.

A year later, Galileo constructed an improvement upon these pioneer implements, and saw with it the satellites of Jupiter, the rings of Saturn and the phases of Venus.

Other inventors rapidly offered improvements upon the telescope; but it was found almost impossible to gain magnifying power, in viewing distant objects, without fringing them with strong prismatic colors produced by the refraction of the rays of light in the lenses of the instrument.

At length the problem was solved by the device known as the reflecting telescope.

James Gregory, of Aberdeen, invented the first reflecting telescope about the year 1666. He died before completing it. Sir Isaac Newton took up the idea, and completed the first reflecting telescope which was ever used in studying the heavens. It magnified forty times, and brought into view the satellites of Jupiter and the phases of Venus. It was about six inches in length, and would be considered a very poor instrument now. But it led the way to investigations and discoveries, whereby he demonstrated his theory of universal gravitation, explained the tides, gave new ideas as to the shape of the earth, and in the following century mathematicians completed the lunar theory which Newton began.

In 1718, Hadley constructed a telescope with 230 magnifying power. In 1785, Sir Sohn Herschel completed his celebrated reflector. In 1824, Joseph Fraunhofer finished the famous telescope for the observatory at Dorpat. And it was not until 1860 that Steinheil found and overcame the practical difficulty in the construction of telescopes.

As far back as 1729, however, an Englishman named Hall, guided by a study of the mechanism of the eye, was led to a plan of combining lenses so as to produce an image free from colors. The secret of their construction died with him. In 1741, Euler regained the lost art by referring to the construction of the human eye; and it is a remarkable fact that almost every successful mechanical contrivance is modeled after some natural mechanism: the shape of the duck for boats; the shape of the bird's wing for kites; the shape of the ear for instruments of sound; and so on.

With the improvements in telescopes came a new insight into the works of nature. "The earth moves!" exclaimed Galileo. Superstition turned upon him like a savage beast. "Take it back," said the powers that were. "Certainly," said he; but to the initiated he whispered, "Still she moves!"

Sir Isaac Newton half a century later, and Leibnitz about the same time, taught men how to prove beyond all cavil, not only that it moves, but that it whirls through free space with inconceivable velocity—calculable in figures, but beyond the wildest imagination.

It was now that men could study nature. It was now they had something to study it with. Men of science—and that too, men of vast mathematical acquirements, supplemented by the highest mechanical skill—proved to be the great students of nature.

Sir Isaac Newton, the discoverer of the binomial theorem, was first to complete a telescope that read the stars aright.

Herschel, the organist of Bath, became musician of the spheres. Such men were scholars first; then mechanics; then interpreters of nature to weaker souls.

The milky-way stood revealed to all mankind

as a congregation of stars, invisible to the naked eye, but palpable forever afterwards to the humblest lover of nature.

It seems strange that men were so long occupied in ascertaining facts which are now so familiar to our school-children.

It was only in the year 1610, that Galileo discovered the satellites of Jupiter. About seventy years earlier, Copernicus had asserted that Venus revolved around our sun. But the followers of Aristotle said that could not be true; for if such were the case, there would be phases like those of the moon. He replied that he had no doubt it would some day be found so. The telescope, which he had been too early to enjoy, verified his prediction. The phases of Venus settled forever the ancient doctrine that the earth was the centre of the universe. The satellites of Jupiter and of other planets subverted the doctrine that the earth was the only planet having a moon revolving about it.

Bacon, in the second aphorism of his *Novum Organum*, has said: "Neither the naked hand, nor the understanding left to itself, can effect much. It is by instruments and helps that the work is done, which are as much wanted for the understanding as for the hand."

Aided by the telescope, science found the sun to be the focus of a planetary system: that Mercury was nearest to it; then Venus; then the Earth; then Mars; then Jupiter; then Saturn; then Uranus; then Neptune; then others—and that these planets moved in elliptic orbits with velocity varying according to certain laws, and not in circles, or with uniform velocity as Ptolemy had supposed.

By the aid of the telescope it was demonstrated that the earth was not a sphere, but a spheroid flattened at the poles. That our sun is only one of a hundred millions of suns that are visible, without counting those too remote to be seen. That our solar system is only one of a hundred millions of solar systems, so distant from us that the nearest of these suns, or fixed stars, as they are called, requires ages for its light to reach us, although light travels at the rate of about 193,000 miles per second. That all these numberless suns, with their attendant worlds, are sweeping through

space with such inconceivable velocity as to baffle
and bewilder the imagination; and that their
movements are regulated with such exact precision, that the close student of nature can foretell
with unerring certainty, for centuries beforehand,
to the fraction of a second, the moment of time
at which a shadow will fall, or a heavenly body
appear, at a given point in its wonderful path of
fire.

The ancients supposed the milky-way to be an
old disused path of the sun. When Herschel
turned his more than magical instrument upon
the silvery belt, he counted between five and six
hundred stars without moving his telescope.

"In a space of the zone, not more than ten degrees long by two and a half degrees wide, he
computed no fewer than 258,000."

Into the same magnificent region Schroeter, of
Lilienthal, directed his telescope, and exclaimed
involuntarily:

"What Omnipotence!"

The difficulty of computing the distance to even
the nearest of the fixed stars, as they are called,
was very great. The longest diameter of the

earth's orbit afforded no parallax. No angle of
the value of a second could be found with certainty in the case of any star. It was not until
within the lifetime of some who hear me now
that Professor Bessel, of Kœnigsberg, by the aid
of an extraordinary refracting telescope with a
micrometer capable of dividing an inch into 80,-
000 equal parts, and two parallel spider webs
adjusted across the centre of the field of view, at
last devised a mechanism of such mathematical
minuteness that an annual parallax of the star
61 Cygni was detected of a little more than one-
third of a second of space. With the side and
two angles of this long little triangle, the calcula-
tion could at last be relied upon to find the remaining angle and the other two sides, and the
distance of the star ascertained at six hundred
thousand radii of the earth's orbit, or, in round
numbers, about sixty billions of miles.

Wearied out with trying to grasp such dis-
tances, and such numbers of objects, the mind
longs for home. We return to the earth and its
phenomena ; its atmosphere ; storms ; tides ; volcanoes ; rocks ; rivers ; mountain and valleys ; its

liquid mass of internal fire ; its cool, thin, hard crust; its changing seasons, snows and rains; clouds and shadows ; its minerals and vegetables, and inhabitants.

Here the study of nature is no less exciting, even when we come down to every-day matters— to every leaf, bird, fish, and insect.

Again we are astonished that it should have taken the wisest philosophers of our race so long a time to find out things that every school-boy now knows, and can explain so well.

Just think what numberless multitudes of our ancestors died under the consummate skill of eminent surgeons and physicians, before Harvey —so late as A. D. 1619—discovered the circu lation of the blood. We of to-day can scarcely understand how such a thing should so long have remained unknown.

It was only about the year A. D. 1295, that Marco Polo carried the mariner's compass into Italy. He got it from the Chinese. Where they got it, nobody knows, but it took civilized nations two hundred years more to get across the ocean with it—in search of gold.

How Jason and his Argosy got along it is hard to say. It may be they had some way to reckon their bearings, which became lost—just as men used to lift ponderous stones, make malleable glass, and manufacture steel swords of metal finer than those made now.

The sailor of to-day only needs his quadrant, his compass and a little patch of sky, to know just where he is.

What the telescope did for the students of celestial phenomena, the microscope did for those who studied the minute forms of terrestrial objects, which were too small to be observed by the naked eye. Innumerable armies of insects were found marching to battle against each other upon the rind of a single orange. A drop of water became a sea full of living creatures, with room to spare. Chemical and botanical science assumed new energy. The mysteries and mistakes of imperfect observation gradually yielded to the new revelations, and the infinite grandeur of the celestial bodies, rolling on in solemn wonder through unfathomable space, kept voiceless guard over the perfections of detail observable in the scarcely visible infinitesimals.

The same August Power that set inexorable fetters upon the ponderous motors of the upper realms, was revealed in the operation of those uniform laws of comparative anatomy, physical geography, botany, chemistry, geology, metallurgy, electricity, and all the elements of modern natural philosophy—branches of material science which are still in their infancy, and awaiting and inviting the investigations of " the coming man."

As yet the wonders that have been accomplished are as nothing to those which are to come. As science advances, mystery retreats. The world moves. Humanity grows wiser and better as it becomes better informed, and barbarism and ignorance can never again dominate this earth.

The study of nature develops the love of law and order and utility, and these things refine and dignify the human race, exalt and ennoble the human understanding. Sooner or later the heathen must go to school. His necessities will drive him there, if not his inclinations; and once having rode on a railroad, or talked through a telephone, he will find himself unable to dispense with them.

But aside from mere utility, the study of terres-

trial nature affords an instinctive pleasure to the
heart. The poets have been called the children
of nature, because they have caught inspiration
from sighing winds, lovely landscapes, magnificent mountains, delicate flowers, and spreading
trees. Not so much as philosophers, but as artists they have painted the plumage of birds, the
waving of grain, the grandeur of ocean, and the
insignificance of man.

Byron sings :

There is a pleasure in the pathless woods,
There is a rapture on the lonely shore,
There is society where none intrudes,
By the deep sea, and music in its roar:
I love not man the less, but Nature more,
From these our interviews, in which I steal
From all I may be, or have been before,
To mingle with the Universe, and feel
What I can ne'er express, yet cannot all conceal.

Roll on, thou deep and dark blue ocean—roll,
Ten thousand fleets sweep over thee in vain ;
Man marks the earth with ruin—his control
Stops with the shore—upon the watery plain
The wrecks are all thy deed, nor doth remain
A shadow of man's ravage, save his own
When for a moment, like a drop of rain,
He sinks into thy depths, with bubbling groan.
Without a grave, unknelled, uncoffined, and unknown.

The aspects of nature are indeed a solace to the eye and a comfort to the heart.

Weary toilers in the field look about them unconscious of fatigue, as they revel in the beauty of the scene. The house-imprisoned toilers of the town, long for fresh air, and a ramble over rock, river and glen. The student of science comes back to his work with fresh hope and vigor, after looking upon the face of nature. The student of art gains all his inspiration there, and as he is true to nature, he becomes gifted in his profession. Creeds, races, nationalities and pursuits may make men differ; but they must all be born, and live and die in nature's lap alike.

"One touch of nature makes the whole world kin."

Who then shall slight this study?

Does it not exalt the mind, comfort the body, and improve the moral and intellectual condition of all? Who is so wise that he does not shudder at his own ignorance, when he begins to realize the countless lessons of nature he has yet to learn!

Life is so short; time is so given to actual business; there are so many impediments to claim attention, that most men will not even take time to reflect upon the nature of things, or they are too sluggish to make themselves comfortable the little time they do have on earth. Entertaining an undue and exaggerated opinion of himself, and his race, and his little third-rate planet, man struts on into his grave, the most inflated, arrogant, pretentious, contradictory insect that creation has fitted for microscopic study.

Dependent upon a thousand accidents and escapes, for even one hour of existence, he proudly assumes the sceptre of immortality. Slave as he is to appetite, sleep, thirst, delusion, disease and death—bondman to each one of a multitude of fierce and debasing passions, he calls himself a sovereign, and assumes to be the arbiter of his own destiny, and able to carve out his own career.

Conscious in his inmost soul of his infirmities, and helplessness, he exults over the weakness of his fellow man; and, forgetting his own frailty, he condemns others for the same faults which he excuses in himself. He cannot exist without food, air, water, and rest. Too cold—he dies; too hot—he perishes; too old—he forgets everything. How diverting it is, then, to see such a dwarf atom in the scale of actualities set up his judgment against the wisdom of the Infinite Creator! He cannot make his own heart beat. He cannot manufacture a grain of wheat or a living leaf. He cannot, by any skill of his, breathe life into matter!

Professor Tyndall, by a serious of brilliant experiments, has demonstrated that the vital principle is not spontaneous even in the smallest and humblest orders of organic matter. In the analysis of atoms, as in the survey of grandeur in the heavens, and sublimity in the ocean, the creative touch remains alone in the finger of God.

Whether man may plume himself in his egotism as a creature of high rank in the scale of intellectual beings, we know not; for we only know the inhabitants of this planet, and the probabilities are strongly in favor of other inhabited worlds.

The plain truth is, we know so little at last that it would be far better to turn our attention to such things as we are permitted to know, and master them, without straining our puny intellects in hopeless aspirations after the unknowable in nature. There are things we can know. There are things we can do. There are fields we can explore. There are duties to humanity we can perform. There are manifestations of the Divine will we can understand. There are truths we can comprehend. With what humility great souls have generally done their work in this world! How simple were their words, and how patient their toil as they taught almost without knowing that they were teaching mankind!

Even so it is given to us to toil on, and humbly do our part, within our little capacity and limited opportunities.

That man is a hero, who bravely, industriously and honestly does the best he can. His name may not figure in the bulletins of rank or fame, but he has done his duty, and the reward of that duty will be to enter at last into the rest of God.

Last summer, in straying along the shore of a bright little lake in Minnesota, I picked up some beautiful little agates. In all St. Louis, with its boasted half million of people, I could only find one man who could polish these stones, and that man refused to do so under my personal inspection and direction, on the ground that his art is a secret mystery which he will not permit any one to see, lest they should learn to become lapidaries.

Yet you can scarcely walk two blocks from his shop without meeting scores of able-bodied loungers, who will beg as medicants, or borrow as knaves, rather than go to work and master a trade, whereby they could secure an honest living.

Our country abounds in crude gems, uncut diamonds, unpolished rubies, opals, emeralds, garnets, topazes, amethysts, and other precious stones—which are worthy to be keepsakes for the living, heir-looms for posterity. Who is working them up? Nobody.

Young men who imagine themselves well educated and able to do anything, but unable to find anything to do, can benefit themselves and others by ascertaining unknown and undetected poisons. The earth, the air, the water, the leaves and vines, all the vegetable and mineral kingdoms, abound in deleterious and oftentimes fatal poisons. What is malaria? What caused epizootic a few years ago among the horses in this country? Why did the best doctors we had perish last year, trying to

find the nature, cause and cure for yellow fever?
The wise man is yet to come who can answer
these questions.

I could go on to give other instances of the un-
developed industries which are all around us, like
gold in the quartz, and zinc in the black-jack, or
blende, glass in the sand, porcelain in the clay,
and salt in the sea ; but time and proper limits to
an address, which is not intended as a lecture,
forbid.

This branch of our State University is instituted
in the right direction. In due time it is destined
to bring rich revenues to the commonwealth. It
is from such seats of learning the naturalists,
the discoverers, the inventors, the observers of
nature must come. It is far better to educate and
refine, enlighten, inform and enrich the people we
have already, and those who in the course of nature will be born to us, than to be yearning for
the wholesale immigration to our State of people
who, when they get here, will not exalt the average standard of our civilization. It is far better
to elevate the moral and intellectual standard of
the people we already have, and make them con-

tented where they are; make them progressive
and law-abiding; make them intelligent and useful citizens, so that at home or abroad, to be
known as a Missourian will be considered as
equivalent to belonging to the higher brotherhood
of educated mankind, worthy of the favored age
in which we live, and welcome as instructors and
companions for the good and the honest people
throughout the world.

The achievements of science are measured by
their practical application to the necessities and
comforts of life. Our State can be benefited by
opening to our rising generation the flood-gates
of general knowledge. Arm them with the
weapons of progress, and they will go on with
good and great works. The books are open to all.
Science is no longer occult. If it is mastered only
by the few, it is not the fault of our institutions,
or of our legislature. It is because only the few
have the fortitude, the patience, the inclination to
devote themselves to noble study. The State can
encourage, has encouraged, and does encourage
this inclination. But it cannot create the inclination. It cannot tutor the unwilling mind. It

cannot guide the indolent hand. It can only leave men free to pursue such avocations as they may prefer with the enjoyment of that high libberty which all recognize as the true liberty, the right to do, to think, to speak, and to write as they please, so they do not trespass upon the rights and the liberties of others.

No fairer field was ever open to rightful ambition, to honest toil, or to useful enterprise.

It is only necessary to feel the inclination to do something, and to acquire the knowledge and skill to do it well. The time for half-way work is past. Men and women have to know what they are about. They must form habits of close observation, and devote all their general knowledge to perfecting the success of whatever special engagement they may undertake. Division of labor has come. The "jack at all trades" has no trade at all.

The success of mechanical invention in the United States is undoubtedly due, in a great measure, to the general diffusion of mathematical knowledge among the people.

Whatever may be said of the advancement of

general learning, or of the standard of literary excellence, it must be conceded that our educational institutions have maintained a high degree of discipline and instruction in mathematical pursuits. The practical application of these studies in manhood, the rich rewards that are open in every direction in a growing country for those who can devise time-saving and labor-saving appliances, have stimulated native ingenuity to its highest exertion; and as one improvement suggests another—and another—the progress of mechanical skill in America has been without a parallel in the history of the world.

And yet we have reason to believe that this department of thought is in its infancy.

There is room everywhere for new invention. The busy brain of the operator and the machinist discerns each day a new necessity that becomes mother to a new invention. The workman should be himself a mathematician and a chemist. The advantage is apparent.

Cheer up, brave young man! ready to despair over problems in Algebra and propositions in Geometry, which seem to you destitute of utility.

Cheer up! and rally once more to your plodding
task. It is through just such trials and sufferings that all great minds have become disciplined
for the labors which have benefited mankind.
It is not for yourself alone. You belong to
society, and you owe to it the exertion of your
best expanded powers. A man amounts to what
he can accomplish for others—not what he can
accomplish for himself alone.

Cheer up! and never despair! Be patient,
but do not wait. Work! Study! Think! Labor!
Exercise! Make an athlete of yourself, and
never fear that the occasion will not arise when
the demands upon you will be greater than all
the strength and ingenuity your discipline and
training can give you. Quicken the faculties of
your mind by dealing with the problems before
you. Acquaint yourself with the problems that
other men have solved. Then take up the train
of thought where they have had to leave it off,
and add to the coral reef your own contribution.
It may be small; but by and by, so built upon,
it will rise above the waters of ignorance and
sluggishness, like rugged cliffs above the rage-
wasting breakers of the sea.

But mere utility in this life is not the highest aim of human study. The intellect that peers through and beyond solar systems for "a sky beyond the cloud, and a star beyond the sky," bends with keen gaze and quenchless longing its glance towards *immortality*. Mere physical existence is not enough. It is too restricted. Through educated faith men look beyond, and yearn for an existence for the soul as infinite in duration as the spaces beyond our physical vision are measureless in extent. Nature shows us the chrysalis. Its form changes. Its identity remains. Its life—goes on.

Revelation shows us the resurrection. The change is not more incredible.

There is no conflict between natural religion and revealed religion. Those who imagine they detect such conflict are simply defectively informed. They do not know all the facts. They cannot comprehend those they do know. Nature has to be observed more attentively. Revelation has to be studied more carefully. When both are understood, both are harmonious.

The profoundest masters of all the sciences

which have lifted the veil of terror and of mystery from nature have been humble believers in the revealed will of God.

The believers in revealed religion cannot justly be charged with superstition. The greatest reasoners, thinkers and teachers of every science, have arisen from their sublime meditations and discoveries with fresh testimony to the moral beauty and dignity of those principles which are so plainly declared in the Scriptures, that a way-faring man, though a fool, need not err therein.

"What Omnipotence!" exclaims the renowned astronomer, as he gazes into the immense vault of the heavens, and realizes that his mind is overwhelmed with a sense of its utter inadequacy to grasp the remotest conception of the awful majesty, wisdom and power of the Almighty Creator.

"What Omnipotence!" echoes the humble believer, who arrives at the same impressions by simply accepting the comprehensive truths of the Bible. The God of Nature, as found by the astronomer, is the same for all practical purposes as the God of the Bible.

A superficial astronomer might be disposed to
pronounce the whole solar system a failure, be·
cause he could detect spots upon the sun. The
wise astronomers know they are there. The sil-
liest of mankind can become actual experts in
carping at the religion of the Bible. It is no
mark of wide thought. Very casual observers
can discern some spots upon the sun.

Yet doth the sun shine on—flinging down life
and light upon the earth, lighting the head-long
pathways of his planets; flooding a grand portion of universal space with radiance; penetrat·
ing, vivifying, comforting, healing, gilding the
twilight clouds with purple glory, and anon waking the birds to songs of melody, and the dewy
rose to sweetness.

And even so, after centuries of "spot-search-
ing" by skeptics, doth the "Sun of Righteous-
ness" shed moral radiance upon mankind, making virtue lovely; home, dear and peaceful; justice, venerable; gratitude, noble; divine love, at-
tainable; faith, inspirational; charity, commend-
able; death, contemptible; cowardice, impossible—painting the cold gray mists of parting life

with the rainbows of Hope; robing old age in the sunset drapery of golden skies; and soothing even the darkness of the shadow of Death with an unfaltering trust and reliance upon Him who doeth all things well!

What God decrees, child of His love,
Take patiently, though it may prove
The storm that wrecks thy treasure here;
Be comforted: thou needst not fear
    What pleases God.

The wisest will, is God's own will,
Rest on this anchor and be still;
For peace around thy path will flow.
When only wishing here below
    What pleases God.

The truest heart is God's own heart,
Which bids thy grief and fear depart;
Protecting, guiding, day and night,
The soul that welcomes here aright
    What pleases God.

Then let the crowd around thee seize
The joys that for a season please,
But willingly their paths forsake,
And for thy blessed portion take
    What pleases God.

Thy heritage is safe in Heaven,
There shall the crown of joy be given;
There shalt thou hear, and see and know,
As thou couldst never here below,
What pleases God.

THE STUDY OF ART.

In a former address delivered before this branch of our State University, it was my privilege to submit some remarks upon the Study of Nature. Your indulgence is now asked to a few observations upon the Study of Art.

Study of any kind is ennobling. It is a struggle for increase of intellectual power. It is a step forward. It is effort for superiority—not over others, but over self. He who studies truly, studies to ascertain something that is not already known. And yet he has studied well who has acquired a small part of that knowledge which "Learning with her ample page, rich with the spoils of time," is ready to impart. To study truly is to read, to listen, to comprehend, to know, to do, and then to teach. The main purpose of a liberal education is to learn how to study.

When this art of study is once mastered, and the faculties are disciplined to its exercise, there are no limits to the activities or the ingenuity of the human mind.

The study of Universal Nature lifts the mind to infinite and sublime contemplations. The study of art unlocks the mysterious doors of knowledge which would otherwise remain impenetrable. Before exploring nature, one should master many arts. Before mastering any art, the oracles of nature must be consulted again and again.

All schools of philosophy agree in the theory that the prehistoric condition of the human race was rude and barbarous.

Men found subsistence in the chase, and in spontaneous fruits, herbs and vegetables. At a later period they lived upon their flocks and the crudest agriculture.

The vestiges of primitive existence, which reach farthest back in time, afford evidence that the art of Pottery was probably the first which engaged the ingenuity of men. Weapons of the chase and of warfare were necessarily of early contrivance. * * A writer has said that a gentleman of that early period would walk out of his cave in the morning, armed with a club, to kill a snake or a frog for his breakfast, which he would eat raw, until his wife and children, who amused themselves in his absence by making mud pies, discovered that clay baked in the sun would hold water, and from that all the earthen cooking utensils and decorated china and porcelain had their start.

It is natural to infer that men studied self-preservtion before they did comfort, and comfort before they did ornament, and that the things which were necessary for existence were studied before the things which afforded ease, and the things which afforded ease before the things which were merely decorative, and the things which were decorative before the things which were ideal. But it is almost certain that the useful as well as the ornamental arts had humble beginnings, and oftentimes accidental origin. Hieroglyphics were used before letters, and letters were used for thousands of years before the invention of printing, and printing was known

as an art long before its magic power was fully
realized. Little by little, step by step, art has
grown from the symbol of the savage to the signal of the electrician.

From feeble beginnings and art without a master, men advanced in knowledge, paused, pondered, plodded—advanced again, and again went
on to the mastery—little by little, step by step.
Almost everything was a mystery at first. With
superstitious awe the ancients enclosed the spot
that had been struck by lightning, because they
thus would mark the place whereon had fallen
the wrathful thunderbolt of Jove. Their solemn
proceeding would appear very ridiculous to a
modern telegraph operator whose hand is accustomed to dally with electricity as a useful toy.
Little by little, step by step — from the kite-
string of Franklin to the wire of Morse, and the
miracles of Edison—little by little, step by step,
science has discovered, and art has utilized dis-
covery, until all mystery has vanished, and the
phenomena of nature demonstrate with unerring
and mathematical conclusiveness the existence
of a skillful and intelligent Creator. The works

of art are the works of man. The works of nature are the works of God.

The study of art is in its infancy. What has been done is only an incentive to further study, and a proof of what study can do.

When one visits a zoological garden, and sees how the brutal strength of the blood-thirsty tiger and the roar of the raging lion are converted into a mere amusement for the children of civilized man, it seems a long way back to that period of humble intelligence, on the part of our ancestors, when such stupid wild beasts were allowed to ravage and lay desolate whole areas of country and fill their inhabitants with terror. Physically, one man is no more able to grapple with one of these monsters now than then; but by means of those agencies of destruction and defense, and appliances for asserting the dominion of mind, which are now employed, brute force is rendered impotent, and becomes even pitiable in the relentless grasp of intellectual power.

How haughtily the elephant must have sneered at the first trap! How the lion must have roared at the first cage! How the panther must have

screamed as it beat the bars of its first prison!
How the leviathan must have splurged and
spouted and lashed the bosom of the mighty
deep at the first hook!

Little by little, step by step, men found something more to subdue than beasts of the field and
monsters of the deep. There must be shelter
from the storm. There must be safety from the
flood. There must be shade from the fiery rays
of the summer sun, and refuge from the winter's
frosts. There must be home, an abiding place
for the family, where the sick could be nursed,
the helpless nurtured, the aged cherished, and
the weary find rest. The torrent must be re-
sisted, the river must be bridged, and the spray-
fringed billows of the ocean must be traversed.
The brute strength of savage men, bent upon
conquest and destruction, must be met and dealt
with as the brute strength of savage beasts. And
after peace had been conquered by the superior
implements of warfare and the dauntless brain of
superior generalship, the arts of war must then
be followed by the far more philosophical arts of
peace. There must be agriculture. There must

be contrivances for storing up supplies against hunger and thirst. There must be store houses. There must be raiment. And when all these are provided, when there is no longer dread of beast or monster, or savage foe, or flood, or storm, or hunger or cold, there must be something to do, there must be something to think—there must be occupation for the brain and for the hand. What has been gained must be preserved and transmitted to posterity, that they might begin where their fathers had left off, and move forward in the grand march of human progress to the music of human ambition for a higher destiny.

It was the mission of art to rescue perishable things from destruction and decay, and make them endure; to snatch dying things from death, and make them live; to portray or carve out beautiful things and make them for monumental memories, fadeless from generation unto generation; to perceive an angelic form captive in a block of stone, and cut it out; to fasten some fleeting thought on canvas, that it might dwell again in other minds and revive a sense of beauty in other ages and for eyes unborn; to create some strong ideal resembling in its imaginative production the inventive faculties of God himself, and thereby realize that man was indeed made in the image of his maker; to inspire the beholder with sentiments of undying glory and immortal fame; to imbue the bosoms of those whose ephemeral existence mocked their vain longings for immortality with patient but confiding hope for life beyond the grave, and impart to the heart bowed down with woe a tender consciousness of Heavenly love, reigning supreme over and above and beyond the sorrows of this earth.

Science may be said to reside in the brain. It has its home in mere intellect. Art must be the offspring of brain and hand combined. One may know how a thing ought to be done, and not know how to execute it. And to approach the perfection of art there must be a combination of brain, hand and heart. There must be not only thought, but work. There must be not only work, but skill or craft. There must be not only skill, but there must be a feeling, an imagination,

an earnest meaning in the work that will bring
into exercise every power and faculty that dis-
tinguishes man from the brute creation. Hence
higher civilization has been inseparable from the
cultivation and supremacy displayed in the arts,
which by way of distinction are designated as
the Fine Arts.

To study the history of art is to study the history of civilization, and the history of the human
race—from the foundations of the world.

No one can fathom the sea of antiquity. It is
all conjecture beyond a certain limit. But this
we do know, that there was no such thing as history until the arts of drawing and writing had
progressed sufficiently to enable men to preserve
history. And yet in that remote period men
must have lived, and thought, and suffered, and
fought and struggled, and died, pretty much as
they do now.

There are two generally approved definitions
of art. One looking to the distinction between
the artificial and the natural; the other looking
to the distinction between the artistic and the
scientific. For the purposes of this address, the

word will be used in its widest sense, embracing in the study of art all that concerns the artisan and the artist, and considering the latter as only a refinement upon the other. First in order, therefore, let us consider the art of the mechanic —the man who not only knows something, but knows how to *do* something, and to do it *well*. Science must lead the way, but art must blaze out the path in the march of man through this wilderness world. It should be remembered, therefore, that the study of art, as a whole, embraces both meanings—art as distinguished from nature, and art as distinguished from science.

Theodore Winthrop says :—

"I reverence as much a great mechanic, in degree, perhaps in kind, as I do any great seer into the mysteries of nature. He is a King, whoever can wield the great forces where other men have not the power. And none can control material forces without a profound knowledge, stated or unstated, of the great masterly laws that order every organism, from dust to man, and a man-freighted world. A great mechanic ranks with the great chiefs of his time — prophets, poets, orators, statesmen."

This tribute to the great mechanic is no more than just, and there is due a proportionate share of credit to every man who makes himself the master of a trade. There is nothing in manual industry to dwarf the mental powers. Benjamin Franklin was a printer; Andrew Johnson was a tailor; Peter Cooper was a cabinet-maker; Hugh Miller was a stone-mason; Elihu Burritt was a blacksmith.

And yet philosophy, politics, philanthropy, theology and philology have produced no examples more brilliant or more profound than such men as these—men who began thinking as they began working, at the bench, the hammer, the anvil or the chisel, and studied as they went along. I mention these names among thousands as eminent, because they have lived in our own era. They are not too far off to be known. There is a disposition in this country to under-rate the high esteem in which the mechanic should be held. It is to him we owe the safety of our houses; the vehicles we ride and travel in; the pavements we walk upon; the implements wherewith our food is cooked; the clothes we wear, the table we eat from, and the articles used in serving and taking our meals; the beds we sleep upon; and the very roof over our heads.

To him we owe every comfort, from the knife and fork to the grand piano; to him we owe every improvement in the useful things which have lifted men from the condition of cave-dwellers, to be inmates of the palace. To him we owe the conveniences which make a modern cottage far more habitable than the ancient castle. To him we owe the steam engine; the railway car; the printing and the binding of our books; the instruments with which the surgeon saves a life, and the light-house that warns the sailor from shipwreck.

The mechanic who conscientiously studies the art of his handicraft, abstains from vice, practices industry, and cultivates his mind while resting his body, is a grander example for either prince or peasant than the greatest nobleman who ever inherited estates which the toil of some other man had earned, or which the greed or cunning of some other man had accumulated. Give me the man who has the health, the manhood, and the honesty to earn his own living by being of use to society, and I will wear him in my heart as one of the jewels of its affections, in preference to the most scientific idler who ever hired a substitute to rob the wool from the sheep's back. It is a grand thing to be useful to others—to be a benefactor. The mechanic is a benefactor. It rather improves him to be a student as well.

It is a curious fact, that the most successful contrivances of art have been perfected by imitations of the mechanisms of nature. Take, for instance, the instrument used by the photographer. It is constructed as much as possible after the fashion of the natural eye of animals.

The duck furnishes the best model for a ship or boat. It is the opinion of scientists, that the machine of the future for navigating the air must be discovered by a still closer study of the structure of the wing of the wild fowl.

Wherever nature has solved a mechanical problem by a joint, a tendon, a pulley, a lens, a valve, or a movement, no human ingenuity has been able to achieve more than a successful imitation— and the contriving mind of the inventor realizes at every step that a far more ingenious contriving mind has studied the subject before him, upon a much grander scale, and embracing a widely more general application. The daintiest joints and wings of the insect afford evidences of plan, fitness, harmony, utility—the adaptation of means to an end—in a word, mechanical skill. And yet revolving planets and solar systems sweep with majestic regularity, order and precision, through the yawning realms of infinite and unfathomable space, guided with inexorable precision by the same Almighty hand—directed by the same Almighty mind.

In our own beloved country the mechanic is accorded the highest honors, and so far from being a drawback to preferment, to have been a mechanic is the surest road to wealth and distinction. The bank presidents and railroad kings, and mining magnates, and solid corporation directors, generally begin as plain, humble, honest, careful mechanics. Little by little, step by step, they buy up the stock and own the mill, the factory, the foundry, the railroad, the bridge, and the bank. It is a short step then to the chair of the governor, a senator, or a president.

They can hire lawyers and doctors, and editors, and preachers, and all sorts of college and university graduates to work for them. No country is so deeply indebted to its mechanics as the United States of America. In less than one hundred years of constitutional government, the mechanics of this country have done more to build it up and make it known abroad, and make it rich and comfortable at home, than all the soldiers and sailors, and writers and doctors, and editors and soft-handed tourists put together. The world owes to the American mechanic the cotton gin; the planing machine; the corn planter; the grain mower and reaper; the rotary printing press; the navigation of water by steam; the hot air engine; the sewing machine; the India rubber industry; the machine for the manufacture of horse shoes; the sand blast for carving; the gauge lathe; the grain elevator; the machine for manufacturing ice on a large scale; the sleeping car for railways; the electric magnet; the telephone, and the electric light.

The mechanics of this country read and think, and keep up with the times. Their genius for practical utility is the wonder of the whole world. They are no mopers and dreamers, but downright workers, and they study mechanical art to such direct purpose, that through their industry and their inventions they have become the practical redeemers of the heathen and the teachers of all mankind. The ship of the merchant carries the missionary of the cross, and the pictures of civilization. The sailor and the manufacturer are the pioneer teachers of all the world, and the extension of commerce means the diffusion of light and knowledge wherever the trader may go.

Let us now take a glance at that division of our subject which relates to the study of art in its more refined and ornamental signification. We are so accustomed to the comforts of life, which are due to the study of mechanical art, that we long for something more. When the immediate wants of existence are supplied, we begin to suffer for imaginary necessities. The soul must have food as well as the body. The disposition must be assuaged, or else melancholy and gloom will settle down like spectres at the bounteous board, and mar the appetite for life.

Pictures and statues make us dwell in the future and in the past, and thus prolong existence. They make us conscious of infinite duration, and thus we realize that the soul within us is immortal.

The study of fine arts, as they are called by way of distinction, leads us up and up, little by little, step by step, until we stand in view of the sublime, the beautiful, the infinite, the everlasting. The use of light and shade, of lines and colors, of form and proportion, in order to impart impressions and feelings, rather than distinct ideas, may be called the instrumentalities of art. But they are not art itself. Art is the force behind them. True art combines the energy of invention with the skill which discerns beauty as in a bright vision, and transfixes it to canvas, or carves it out of stone so faithfully, that others may find the soul of which that beauty was born by gazing upon the external form. The copying of form is only the foundation of real art. Carving preceded drawing; sculpture preceded painting. The first artists dealt with images of forms. Then followed successive advances from images to ideas, and art became ideal rather than formal. Thenceforward art signified the material expression, not only of thought, but of emotion. Architecture, the grandest of all arts, because it embraces and finds room for all, stimulated the sculptor and the painter to nobler and loftier designs. The genius of man laid hold upon the solid rock, making a marble Venus almost breathe with passion; a marble Milo almost roar with pain; a marble Laocoon almost melt with agony and despair.

Whether architecture grew from the mound to the pyramid; from the pyramid to the temple; from the temple to the palace in India, or Arabia, or Assyria, or Egypt, must ever remain in dispute. But certain it is that it grew, and that it grew by small degrees.

Cadmus is said to have carried letters into Greece about the year 1400 before the Christian era.

That older civilizations found means to preserve written history before that, there is abundant evidence.

But the most we can gather from such remote

antiquity becomes of secondary importance to the student of art. It is a labor ending in the gratification of mere curiosity. It is enough for practical purposes to know that little by little, step by step, art grew from the pottery of the mound builders to the obelisks of Egypt, the as yet unequalled statues of Greece, and the awe-inspiring frescoes of Rome—"the eternal city that sat upon her seven hills, and from her throne of beauty ruled the world."

Whenever a nation grew strong and warlike, and pushed its conquests into the territory of older and richer countries, the spoils that were always carried away with the greatest zeal were the celebrated works of art. Out of the cruelties and hardships of war humanity found at least this consolation, that the arts and refinements of the conquered people achieved a sort of victory over the conquerors.

Religious fervor imbued its devotees with certain tastes and inspirations that gave tone to the style of architecture, and of sculpture and painting, which prevailed among the various peoples of the earth, and the philosophy of art became tinged everywhere by the customs, habits and religious beliefs of the peculiar people from whom the artists had their origin.

The learning and the arts of the East and of Egypt went to Greece, from Greece to Rome, from Rome to Western Europe, and from Western Europe to America—the land reserved by Heaven to be the last and best home of the arts, as it is the last and best home of philosophy, learning, science and civil government, founded upon principles of constitutional liberty. There never has existed a time or a place in the history of the world so auspicious for the student of art as this country at the present time.

Men are amassing fortunes; the National and State governments are erecting great public buildings; education is cherished as the pearl of great price; refined taste is cultivated at home, and enriched by swift and luxurious trips around the world; the arts of engraving and photography have made those who have never traveled familiar with all the most admired and celebrated works of art in every part of the world; and there is no reason why the American architect. the American engineer, and the American artist should not achieve, as well as the American mechanic, the highest honors which the world can lavish upon genius. The time is at hand when these things must follow as a natural sequence of the wonderful progress our country has made in every field of intellectual development and material resources.

When Phidias, the greatest of the Greek sculptors, had completed his masterpiece, a statue of Athena, which was massively inlaid with ivory and gold furnished by the State, he was falsely accused of having appropriated some of the expensive materials to his own use. In order to refute his accusers, he asked that the costly material be taken from the statue and weighed. This they refused to do, and yet, actuated by political animosity towards Pericles, who was the friend and patron of Phidias, they caused him to be cast into prison, where, stung to death by their ingratitude, he languished and died.

The genius of Michael Angelo Buonarotti was fettered by political persecution the better portion of his life; and the personal biography of nearly every great artist discloses a story of patient apprenticeship, terrible labors, mortifying neglect, the envy of rivals, and the harsh injustice of critics. And yet there is such a fascination in the study of the fine arts, that the sorrows and vicissitudes of the artist's life have been borne with the heroic fortitude and resignation of martyrdom itself. The true student of art has incessant occupation, infinite sources of thought, grand day dreams, endless invention, exquisite accuracy; and when fame and fortune do smile, there is such a triumphant looking forward to future renown, that ambition for undying glory nerves the trembling hand, thrills the swelling vein, and assuages the throbbing heart. Science consists in knowing, but art consists in doing. And whoever has the wisdom to learn, the capacity to understand, the invention to design, the art to execute, and the patience to labor, will realize that in the study of art there are fountains of more unfailing joy than in any pursuit which can engage the faculties and stimulate the energies of man.

The cultivation of taste for the fine arts has

lately received a powerful impetus in our own
State, by the dedication to public use of a magnificent building, a Museum of Fine Arts, by Mr.
Wayman Crow, at St. Louis. There will be
gathered the art treasures which are to embellish
and characterize our civilization. There the student of art will find the masterpieces of great
artists; and let us hope that its enduring walls
will be enriched by gems of beauty that slumber
now within the soul of some Missouri boy, as yet
" to fortune and to fame unknown."

YOUTH.

There are gains for all our losses,
    There are balms for all our pain ;
But when youth—the dream—departs,
It takes something from our hearts,
    And it never comes again.

We are stronger, we are better,
    Under manhood's sterner reign ;
Still we feel that something sweet
Followed youth, with flying feet,
    And can never come again.

Something beautiful is vanished,
    And we sigh for it in vain :
We seek it everywhere—
On the earth and in the air—
    But it never comes again.

June 5, 1878.